CAPTURED

CAPTURED

TRIONI HARRISON

Captured

This book is written to provide information and motivation to readers. Its purpose is not to render any type of psychological, legal, or professional advice of any kind. The content is the sole opinion and expression of the author, and not necessarily that of the publisher.

Copyright © 2020 by Trioni Harrison.

Printed in the United States of America.

ISBN   978-1-951913-31-1   (Paperback)
ISBN   978-1-951913-32-8   (Digital)

Lettra Press books may be ordered through booksellers or by contacting:

Lettra Press LLC
30 N Gould St. Suite 4753
Sheridan, WY 82801, USA
1 303-586-1431 | info@lettrapress.com
www.lettrapress.com

Mission Statement

Captured is a riveting, compelling story of a young woman who became disillusioned with love, but after meeting that special someone, she understood why it didn't work with Adam, whom she'd originally presumed to be the love of her life.

****

"Men can't be trusted."

Andy was humming softly to herself as she worked on her design when her private line rang. She lifted the receiver to the sultry voice of Dandre'. "Hello, beautiful. How are you?"

"Hi, Dandre'. I am wonderful. And you?"

"I am doing much better because I've heard your lovely voice," he said, chuckling. "How about dinner and a movie tonight?"

"I'm sorry, Dandre', but I must decline your offer. As I told you before, I am not interested in dating."

"And why is that?" he asked.

"I am really busy with my career right now. Besides, I don't think it's a good idea."

"I see," he said.

Andy's heart was beating so fast it felt like it was about to jump out of her chest.

"What are you afraid of? he asked. "Is having dinner with me that bad?"

"Who said I was afraid?" she countered. "Men can't be trusted, and I have neither the time nor the inclination to get into another dead-end relationship."

> Let him kiss me with the kisses of his mouth
> for your love is better than wine.
>
> —Songs of Solomon 1:2

To my friend Lorraine Aycock, who has been a tremendous support throughout this whole process. Thank you for listening to me as the characters became a reality. I love you so very much.

Twelve Major Keywords

spellbinding
riveting
electrifying
hot
alluring
compelling
intense
passionate
epic
Jamaica
thrilling
irresistible

ABOUT THE AUTHOR

Donna Johnson is a native of Jamaica. She read her first Mills & Boon at the age of sixteen, and since then she's continued to read anything she can find. As a child growing up, she always believed in fairy tales and happily ever after. As an avid reader, she borrowed dozens of books from the local library every week. With a flair for the dramatic, she wrote her first play for her high school drama group, *Endless Love.*

She went to college and graduated with a degree in finance. She worked in banking for many years before resigning from her position to work in public schools as a teacher. Her love for reading and passion for writing, coupled with the encouragement of family and friends, led her to pen her first love story. She now writes romance novels under the pen name Trioni Harrison.

Donna resides in Atlanta, Georgia, and spends her time with her family and friends.

CHAPTER 1

Anjou reached over to the nightstand to turn off the alarm clock. As she did, she groaned, "Oh Lord. It can't be morning already." She wished she could close her eyes for a few more minutes before getting out of bed. As she threw the covers back and sat up in bed, her mind began to go over the list of different projects for the day. She padded from the bedroom of her condo to the kitchen and made a cup of Blue Mountain coffee. The rich, fragrant smell of brew soothed her tired nerves, and the warmth of the drink seeped into her cold fingers as they closed around the cup. She sipped her coffee, refusing to let her mind dwell on the nightmare she'd had last night or on the past.

She had taught herself to ignore the past. OK, so she could not erase it, could not entirely put it behind her and close the door on it. But she could resist the temptation to dwell obsessively on it. When she had returned from Kingston, she had vowed to put it behind her. She had fought vigorously and valiantly against a sense of insecurity and inadequacy. She was doing great now. Something must have happened in her subconscious mind to trigger the nightmares again.

Andy reminded herself that she was successful in her own right. She had bought her condo just a few short months after joining her family-owned business. She had come out from behind the shadows of her ex-fiancé, or so she had told herself. But did one really recover wholly from the trauma of a broken engagement? Wasn't it true that somewhere deep inside she had considered herself inferior and unworthy, judging herself as Adam 's parents had done simply because her skin was not the same colour as theirs?

"Stop that!" she admonished herself, pushing away from the kitchen counter and walking towards the bathroom. She was wide awake now and might as well get moving. She had a very busy morning ahead of her. There was a meeting scheduled at 9.30 with one of the firm's biggest clients. The chief draughtsman for Wilson & Wilson Architecture could be very demanding. But it was easier said than done, which accounted for the fact that the past still haunted her in the form of tormenting nightmares, even after all this time.

The company was formed by her great grandfather and his brothers, and it had been in business for more than sixty years. Andy prided herself on upholding the high standard set by her predecessors, and she vowed to provide the same prestigious service for which the firm was known. The company was contracted by the government and some of Jamaica's wealthiest socialites to design the plan for the largest hospital to be built in Negril. It was an honour, to say the least.

After she showered, she towelled herself dry and regarded her long black hair, ruefully knowing she did not have enough time to do anything with it other than resorting to her famous french twist. After applying moisturiser, a light foundation, a touch of mascara to her long dark lashes, and just a touch of lip gloss to her full lips, she was ready to go. As she stood in the mirror gazing at her reflection, she could hear her grandfather's voice say, "Andy, you look so much like my

Lila." At the thought of her grandmother, a smile touched her lips. Her grandmother was beautiful. The classic bone structure of Grandma Lila's face was astounding. She was often thought of as elegant and classy.

Andy was tall with a slender body and hips, and she had legs to die for, as her sisters often said. Like her mom, she had the most beautiful hazel eyes, high cheekbones, and a caramel complexion. She was one of a set of triplets that was born to her parents, and Andy believed that her sisters were much prettier than her. Not that it mattered. She loved her sisters, Marche and Marconnets. Then there were her three brothers, Andre, Noel, and Nicholas. The six siblings shared a very close bond. The brothers were often thought to be overprotective and overbearing by their sisters.

Andy smiled at her reflection one last time and headed for the door. The classic coolness of her demeanour was in direct contrast to her inner insecurities, but few people could guess that. Not even Jason, who was in hot pursuit of her, saw what she hid so well from public view. Jason! Andy groaned unwittingly, biting her lower lip and thus marring its fullness with her teeth. He had been employed with the company for the last two years, and for the past four months he'd invited her out at least once a week. She liked and admired Jason personally, and physically he was a very attractive man: tall and ruggedly handsome, with a nice smile and easy charm. But when it came to the crunch, when it came to dating him, she held back. She knew he found her coldness towards him hurtful, but how could she explain to him that she was not attracted to him? Or was it still the residue of what Adam had done to her that made her wary of romantic relationships? Adam had become the mental guardian of her morals—had extended far more control that vetoed her ability to respond to the opposite sex.

Stop thinking about that now! she admonished herself for the millionth time. She would need all her faculties and wits about her at this meeting. This was the opportunity of a lifetime for the company. Sighing softly, she collected her things she needed for the day. Andy knew Jason was intrigued by her. He found her sexual coldness a challenge that he was not used to facing. He was used to women throwing themselves at him, and he couldn't see that her refusal to go out or to sleep with him was not a manoeuvre in a clever game but a genuine abhorrence of any form of intimacy on her part.

Andy parked her Escalade in the spot reserved for her at the side of the office building and entered the foyer. The security at the desk greeted her cheerily. "Good morning, Ms Royale."

"Good morning, Bob. How are you doing?"

As she entered her office, the phone began to ring. She hurriedly closed the door and picked up the receiver. Her secretary's voice came over the line. "Ms Royale, your sister Marconnets is on line three."

"Please put her through, Mrs Gray. Hey, sis. What's up?" Andy said.

"Nothing. Just called to remind you of our get-together tonight at 8.00, at Sunset Negril," Marconnets said. "Please tell me you have not forgotten our girl's night out?"

"I have not forgotten," Andy said. "As a matter of fact, I am so glad today is Friday. That means I get to sleep in tomorrow. I am really tired. This project with building the hospital is very demanding. Mr Crosby has already changed the design three times for the cardiac unit because he is the largest donor. He thinks it gives him the right to do so."

"Well, sis, you know the saying: money talks."

"Yep, you are right about that."

The sisters chatted for a few more minutes, and then Andy said, "I should go. I have a 9.30 meeting and would like to review the blueprint."

"OK, I will see you later tonight. Enjoy the rest of your day."

"Thanks, Marconnets. See you later."

Andy looked up from her computer as the clock on the wall chimed 6.00 p.m. *My goodness, where did the time go?* It felt like she'd just left the meeting with her brother Nicholas and the other architects and engineers. Thank God Mr Crosby was finally satisfied with the design for the cardiac unit. It was quite obvious that everyone was at their wits' end with the man. It never ceased to amaze Andy that just because some people were in possession of more money than others, they felt they could have everything they wanted. But then again, the good book did say money answered in all things. The chief of staff at the hospital would oblige Mr Crosby the world; to the man's way of thinking, it would have been worth the compromise for the new cardiac unit.

Andy closed the final window on her computer and hit the power button. As she exited the building, she thought if she made it home by 6.30, she could take a leisurely soak in the bathtub for at least twenty minutes to ease the tension in her neck, shoulders, and back. Sighing, she opened the door of her SUV, started the vehicle, and eased into traffic.

Almost two hours later, Andy, Marche, Marconnets, Paige, Trista, and Gail sat at one of the exclusive tables in the upscale restaurant Sunset Negril. The name *Negril* was the shortened version of *Negrillo*, Spanish for "little black ones", as it was originally named by the Spanish in 1494. The name was thought by some to be a reference to the black cliffs south of the village. Negril was a laid-back town in western Jamaica, and it was known for its miles of uninterrupted white-sand beaches on shallow bays with calm, pale waters. Seven miles of beach, particularly the portion overlooking the Long Bay, were lined with bars, restaurants, and resorts, many of them international and all-inclusive. It was also popular for water sports, and at night reggae and dancehall music emanated from surfside clubs. Negril was a world apart, and the pristine beauty that brought its fame was only a memory, but the magic persisted like a gaudy shell necklace. A conglomeration of tourist facilities covered the coast for fifteen miles from Bloody Bay to the lighthouse, and they continued to grow on both ends. The once deserted Norman Manley Boulevard was a speed track for buses, vans, motorbikes, and taxis. Across the bridge, shopping plazas proliferated, even on the west end, known as the rock, where iron shore cliffs plunged to the turquoise-aquamarine seas.

As the waiter placed their drinks on the table, he enquired, "Would you ladies like to order now?"

Trista said, "Would you give us a few minutes to look at the menu, please?"

"Sure, no problem. I will be back in a few to take your order."

"Oh my goodness. Girl, take a look at the brother who just walked in. He is definitely a good-looking man. A fine work of art sculptured in all the right places."

"Dear Lord, I wonder who the lucky lady is meeting him here? I wish it was me."

Feminine whispers rippled through the restaurant as a number of heads turned, and admiring eyes glanced towards the man entering the establishment. Dandre' Neilson was oblivious to the attention he was getting. His gaze roamed the room before zeroing on the table Anjou and her sisters were sitting at.

Golden eyes locked with hazel eyes, and it seemed to Andy that time stood still. Bolts of electricity shot through her like a warm caress as the stranger stared at her. Andy felt like she had stopped breathing and they were the only two people in the world as time stood still. Just then, the melodious voice of Whitney Houston could be heard singing "One Moment in Time". Andy's heart rate accelerated, and heat of the most intense kind began to pool at the centre of her legs, leaving her gasping for breath.

Dandre' felt the charge of electricity through his body from the top of his head to the soles of his feet. For what seemed like an eternity, he was captivated by the most enchanting creature he had ever laid eyes on. Her hair was blacker than a raven's feather, and as the light shined on it, it looked like long strand of black silk thread. Slowly his eyes travelled to the graceful and delicate column of her neck. Her face was the colour of warm caramel, and she had high cheekbones. Her lips were full and pouting as she tried to breathe. Dandre' felt his lips grow dry, and his manhood became hard as a rock. Suddenly he wished his mystery woman was standing so he could see the rest of her.

He was brought back to reality as the maître d' said, "Welcome to Sunset Negril. Will you be dining alone?"

He glanced down in to the smiling face of the maître d'. "I meeting my brothers here. I believe they made reservations. It should be under Neilson."

The woman's smile widened. "So you are Colar and Chayse's brother?"

"Yeah. I gather you know my brothers?" He knew that most females in Negril were familiar with his brothers, the confirmed bachelors.

A soft chuckle escaped the hostess's mouth. "Oh yes. I know your brothers. Your brothers have not arrived yet, but if you don't mind following me, I will show you to your table." She led him to a table facing the window that overlooked the sea. In the distance, he could hear the gentle lapping of the waves.

As Dandre' followed his hostess, he realised he had to walked by his mystery woman. He felt his heart beat increase, and he wondered what was wrong with him. He told himself it had been too long since he had been intimate with a woman.

"Would you like to order now, or do you want to wait until your brothers get here?"

"I will wait."

"OK. Would you like something to drink while you wait?"

"I would like a glass of club soda on the rocks, please."

"I will be right back," she said as she walked away.

The effects of the handsome stranger did not go unnoticed by Andy's sisters and friends, who turned to her and asked what that was about. Andy replied, "I have no idea what you ladies are talking about."

Gail said, "Come on, Andy. We all have eyes, and we are no fools. You're attracted to Mr Handsome. Ain't nothing wrong with that."

"I think I am ready to order. What do you have a taste for?" Marche asked the others.

Paige said, "I think I will have the codfish fritters as an appetiser. Then I want the jerk chicken salad with steamed dumplings smothered in gravy. For dessert I'll take a slice of sweet potato pudding with vanilla ice cream and a healthy glass of Stones ginger wine."

Andy ordered oxtail with red beans and rice and a Caesar salad with red wine. Gail order lobster tail stuffed with crab meat, with sweet potatoes soufflé and a glass of Chardonnay Trista. Marconnets ordered Italian lasagne, and Marche ordered roast beef with red potatoes served with glazed carrots and a glass of port wine; for dessert, she ordered raspberry cheesecake.

As they waited for dinner to be served, Andy realised that her insides were still shaking with Dandre' sitting across from her table. No one had ever affected her this way. She tried to concentrate on the conversation but found that it was impossible.

As Dandre' waited for his brothers to arrive, he glanced at where his beautiful enchantress was sitting. He then looked at the other women sitting at the table and realised that two of the women had a startling resemblance to his mystery woman. Just then a movement caught his eyes. He saw that his brothers had arrived. Colar, his younger brother, was working the tables by flirting with the ladies as they headed towards him.

Dandre' could not help but muse at how different the four Neilson brothers were. Christopher was the oldest of them, and he was quiet and easy-going. He was a pilot with the JFDF Air Force, and he was happily married to the beautiful Melody Spencer, the daughter of Congressman Karl Spencer. Chayse was chief paediatrician at Sangster General Hospital, and twice a week he volunteered at the local clinic located in the heart of the ghetto. Baby brother Colar owned his own vineyard in the Handover Valley, and he operated orphanages. He was considered the sensitive one and the die-hard womaniser. Dandre' knew he was often considered the most intense, secretive, complex, and outspoken of them all.

"Sorry we are late," Chayse said. "Traffic was hellacious coming from Montego Bay." With a mischievous grin on his face, he sat down.

"So tell me what you think of this place," Colar said, looking at Dandre'. "Have you ever seen so many beautiful women under the same roof? I feel like I have died and gone to girl's heaven."

Dandre' rolled his eyes and picked up his menu. "I am hungry and am ready to order."

Colar leaned back in his chair and surveyed the room. He looked across the table where Andy and her colleagues were sitting, and his eyes rested on Paige. Both Chayse and Dandre' followed the direction of their brother's roving eyes.

"Wow," Chayse said. "Who are those beautiful ladies? I don't believe I have seen any of them before."

Colar said, "Me neither. I would definitely remember if I had."

Dandre' shrugged his massive shoulders. "Your guess is as good as mine."

Colar was halfway out of his chair. "Do you mind if we invited them to join us?"

Dandre' said, "Sit the hell down, Colar. I thought we are here to discuss business."

Colar slowly sat down. "Damn. Yeah, you are right. But before the night is over, I will get that redhead's number."

Dandre' stared long and hard at Colar and snorted in frustration.

"You are hopeless case, Dandre'."

"Does that mean that you're finally giving up on me?"

Colar chuckled. "It would serve you right if I did, but I won't let you off the hook that easily. When was the last time you were with a woman?"

Dandre' frowned. "None of your damned business."

"Ha! It's been that long, huh?" Colar said. "I am your brother, and I love you. I want you to be sexually fulfilled like the rest of us. You need to get laid so you knock off that hard, mean edge."

Chayse chuckled as he watched the intense exchange between his brothers. Chayse turned to Colar and said, "Sometimes I wonder who is the baby."

"You just feel it's your god-given right to mess with other people's lives."

"Yeah," Colar said, laughing. "I am glad I am the baby of the family, because it gives me audacity and the privilege to say whatever I like, and there isn't anything you can do about it."

Dandre' grinned and shook his head. "The last time for me, I am sure, was probably not as recent as for you."

"Probably not," Colar responded, scanning the menu. "So what's the problem?"

"Excuse me?"

"I asked, what's the problem?" Colar repeated.

"There isn't one. Contrary to what you believe, there are more important things in life than sex."

"Oh, is that so?" Colar exclaimed in a voice loaded with disbelief. "Name one."

Dandre' looked at Chayse, and they burst out laughing. Chayse said, "Dandre' may be hopeless, but you are sick, bro. You need some serious help."

Colar grinned. "If I am, you'd better believe I am a very satisfied one. But seriously, I can hook you up, Dandre'."

"Damn, give it a rest," Chayse said to his younger brother. "You just don't know when to quit."

Just then, from the corner of his eye, Dandre' saw Andy and her colleagues were leaving. Dandre' pushed his chair back. "No, thank you. I can find my own woman."

"Hey, where are you going?" cried Colar.

Chayse exclaimed, "The ladies are leaving. I think one of them has caught Dandre's fancy."

Dandre' caught up with Andy as she was exiting the restaurant. He rushed forward to get the door. "Please allow me," he said.

As the ladies walked out into the parking lot, Dandre' walked up to Andy and said, "Hello. My name is Dandre'." He extended his hand to her, and Andy reached out to take it.

Immediately it felt like she was hit with a thousand watts as she placed her small hand in his. As his fingers close around hers, she felt breathless. She said, "I am Anjou, but my friends call me Andy." As she gazed into his eyes, she felt the same sensation she'd had earlier when he'd walked in the restaurant.

He said, "Can I call you sometime? May I have your number?"

A slight tremor went through her at the sound of his voice. Andy looked at the others and read the answer in their eyes: "Yes, girl. Give him your number." She reached in her purse for a business card and handed it to him. She then performed a quick introduction of her sisters and friends.

Dandre' asked if they were all related. Marche answered, "Three of us are triplets, and the rest are friends and cousins."

"Oh," Dandre' said. "It's nice meeting you all. I will give you a call." He watched them get into their respective vehicles.

As Andy headed home, she wondered whether she had

done the right thing in giving Dandre' her number. The last thing she needed was another man chasing after her like a lost puppy. She chuckled to herself and wondered. There must be a sign on her forehead that said, "Come hither."

Andy and her sisters were on their way to a fundraising gala sponsored by Loving Life Foundation, which was engaged in wildlife conservation. Most people were not aware that wildlife was in danger of becoming extinct. Wildlife conservation was the practice of protecting wild plant and animal species and their habitats. The goal was to ensure that nature would be around for future generations to enjoy, and also to recognise the importance of wildlife and wilderness for humans and other species. As the president of the foundation, Andy hoped that different businesses in the community would be generous in their donations. There were so many things that they needed. She was also hopeful that some retired professionals would volunteer their time to do research.

After walking into the grand ballroom of the Sugar Bay Hotel, Andy's heart leapt for joy at the sight that greeted her eyes. The room was packed to capacity, and there were people everywhere. She made her way to front of the room and stopped to chat with some of the guests.

The principal of Morant Bay University stopped her. "Ms Royale, I have been meaning to contact, you but preparing for upcoming exams for our students has kept me quite busy. What I wanted to know is do you need a science professor? If you don't mind, I am available to assist you in any capacity."

Andy was thrilled and replied, "I would be delighted to have you, Mr Mitchell. As a matter of fact, I have just the right project for you." He beamed from ear to ear and handed her a check for a very large donation.

As the evening progressed, businesses and private organizations presented their donations and pledged their continued support. At the end of the gala, Andy was very pleased that it was a success.

The next day, Andy received a call from one of the botanical gardens in Kingston. They were having a conference on environmental control and wanted to know if Andy would be the keynote speaker. Andy was over the moon at the invitation. She liked rare and exotic flowers, and this botanical garden was established in 1873 by Major R. Hope, a British commander. It sat on approximately two hundred acres of land. Attractions at the garden included a palm grove, a cactus garden, an orchid house, and an ornamental pond. This garden attracted over two million visitors per year. Not only did locals enjoy visiting the garden all year round, but it was also a site where numerous wedding took place.

For the rest of day, Andy was kept really busy. There were deadlines to meet, and the company had just taken on a new client who wanted her to design a luxury apartment complex. The specification was that these apartments would be all-inclusive; amenities included a gym, an athletic club, a swimming pool, and a tennis court. It would be the first of its kind and would be located in the heart of downtown Negril.

Andy was humming softly to herself as she worked on the design when her private line rang. She lifted the receiver and heard the sultry voice of Dandre'. "Hello, beautiful. How are you?"

"Hi, Dandre'. I am wonderful, and you?"

"I am doing much better now that I've heard your lovely voice," he said, chuckling. "How about dinner and a movie tonight?"

"I am sorry, Dandre', but I must decline your offer. As I told you before, I am not interested in dating."

"And why is that?" he asked.

"I am really busy right now with my career. Besides, I don't think it's a good idea."

He said, "I see."

Andy's heart was beating so fast that it felt like it was about to jump out of her chest.

"What are you afraid of?" he asked. "Is having dinner with me so bad?"

"Who said I was afraid?" she countered. "Men can't be trusted, and I have neither the time nor the inclination to get into another dead-end relationship. So if you don't mind, I have to go. I have a lot of work to finish before I leave today."

After she hung up the phone, Andy sat at her desk and stared in space as the little voice in her head called her a coward. More than once, she was tempted to accept Dandre's invitation to go out, but the memories of what she'd gone through with Adam brought the bitter taste of bile to her throat and caused her to change her mind. To her way of thinking, pretty boys like Dandre' were usually after only one thing. It was better to steer clear of him. She sighed and turned her attention to the design on which she was working.

CHAPTER 2

Dandre' walked into the living room and threw his car keys on the coffee table. A million thoughts went through his mind. For weeks he had been in a foul mood, and his entire staff avoided him like he had the Ebola virus. They wouldn't even make eye contact with him. He was beginning to feel like an eel. He normally wasn't a grouch, and people loved to work for him. He tried to not take out his frustrations on his staff. Somehow he would have to find a way to make it right.

But at this moment, all he could think about was Anjou. He definitely desired the beautiful Anjou Royale. It was time to implement his master plan. After he'd called her a couple of days ago, she primly informed him, "I don't do relationships," he had asked why. She said, "Men can't be trusted."

With a chuckle, he replied, "I am not most men. Would you allow me to take you out and redeem our species?"

To that, she said, "I can see that, but the answer is still a double no,"

"What the hell is a double no?" He couldn't help but wonder who was the jackass who'd broken her was. The moment he laid eyes on her, he knew she was the one. He had no idea that after finding the one, it would not be smooth sailing. If she need convincing, he was prepared to do more than that.

As the master of seduction, he told himself, "Andy does not stand a chance in hell. Before she knows it, we will be walking down the aisle." He planned to have a boatload of children, and she would be the mother of them all. He could see her with her stomach getting bigger and bigger as she carried his child.

The image did strange things to his insides. Dandre' realised he had it really bad. If his brothers knew what he was thinking, they would never let him live it down. He knew it would be like this when he fell in love—that he would fall hard. The only one who could catch him was Anjou.

Dandre' had dated over the years, but he had never had a thought about a woman having his baby, or even getting married to anyone. His mind went back to Andy. From what he had learned, she had experienced one hell of a broken heart, and she had since sworn off men. To his way of thinking, he simply had to show her that some man came to take, but he came to restore. First he had to get her to fall in love with him.

He remembered his friend Tyler's words. "I hope you know what you are doing. Dealing with Andy will not be a walk in the park."

Dandre' said, "I like a good challenge, and winning Andy's heart will make the victory worth it all." Dandre's expression was serious. "She will fall in love with me. She must. If not, I will spend the rest of my life alone. She is the only one for me. I know it."

To any other woman, Dandre's relentless pursuit would seem like a romantic move, but Tyler was convinced otherwise. You are my friend, and the last thing I would want is that you fall in love with a woman who is incapable of loving you back."

"Don't worry, my friend. I intend to come out smelling like a rose and walking away with the best prize of all—Anjou."

"How do you plan to accomplish such humungous task?" Tyler asked. "Don't you think you're been a little presumptuous? Andy won't even consider going on a date with you."

Dandre' smiled and said, "I have a plan. You will see."

"So have you heard from Dandre'?" Marche asked Andy.

"Yes. He called me a few days ago and asked if he could take me to dinner."

"What did you say?"

Andy replied, "I turned him down."

"You did *what*?" roared Marche.

"You heard me. I turned him down."

"I think you are being unfair to him. When will you forget the past and move on? Will every man have to pay for what Adam did to you?"

"Who said I have not moved on?" I just don't have a heart to give to another man. Besides, I don't have time to date. As you can see, I am very busy with my career."

"I never thought you were a coward," Marche said.

"What is that supposed to mean?" Andy asked.

"That is the lamest excuse, if ever I heard one. You being too busy to date. You are hiding behind your job, and you know it."

Andy chuckled. "No, I am not."

"OK, if you say so."

At that moment, Andy's mind went back in time. She could still remember the last song they had danced to. "Lady, I am your knight in shining armour and I love you. You have made me what I am, and I am yours. My love, there are so many ways I want to say I love you. Let me hold you in my arms forever more." He was holding her so close that she could feel his heart beating against her cheeks. She could still feel the warmth of his breath on her neck as they swayed to the music. He gently whispered, "Your love is the only love I ever need."

Another memory was fresh in her mind. She remembered the last time they were together. She was cooking dinner for him, his favourite meal, when he walked in with a beautiful bouquet of yellow roses. "How pretty," she said, smiling. "Thank you."

"You are welcome." He stared at her as if she was a delicious morsel he wanted to taste.

"Is everything all right?" she asked.

"Yes," he replied. "Why do you asked?"

"Because you are staring at me with an odd expression."

Adam smiled as he wrapped his arms around her. "I am staring because you are the most beautiful lady, and you belong to me. He kissed her then.

"Andy, are you all right?" Marche asked, jolting her out of her reverie.

Andy replied, "Yes, I am fine," with a forced smile on her face. With all the declarations of love, when the rubbers met the roads, that love was not strong enough to endure the pressure from his family. All hell had broken loose when he had announced their engagement.

They had gone to see his father and step-mother. The atmosphere around the dinner table was strained, although his sister and her husband, Charles, did their best to smooth things over. After dinner, everyone had retired to the drawing room for drinks. It was then that Andy had excused herself to go to the ladies' room. As she was about to turn the corner, she heard voices. She stopped, not wanting to interrupt, and she was shocked at what she had heard.

His mother said, "I am telling you, Frederick, there is not going to be a wedding between Adam and Anjou. It will be over my dead body! I have a more suitable wife for him."

"Who is that?" his father asked.

"Judith, of course," his mother said. "She is one of us. Besides, her parents are our business colleagues. Anjou just doesn't belong in our world, and she never will."

Feeling sick to her stomach, Andy backed up so they would not see her. She felt tears of humiliation burning in her eyes. She quickly turned around and ran into Charles. He caught her by the arm to stop her from falling.

"Are you all right, my dear?" he asked.

"No, I am not," she replied. "Please excuse me. I have to go." While wiping the tears from her eyes, she walked out the side door of his parents' home.

In the end, his parents had won. He'd left her and wed another. He was too afraid of been disinherited. It was true the memories no longer hurt, but she no longer trusted men. She had learnt the hard way talk was cheap.

To change the focus of her sister's attention, she asked, "What are you wearing to the governor's ball next week?"

"I have no idea," Marche said. "I was thinking that you, Marconnets, and I could go shopping on Saturday."

"That's a great idea. Let me know what time on Saturday."

After leaving her sister, Andy went into her office to finish up some last-minute drawings for the hospital building. A few hours later, the phone on her desk rang. As she lifted the receiver, she wondered whether she would have the pleasure of designing another hospital.

"Ms Royale, there is a Mr Neilson on line one. Shall I put him through?"

"Yes, please do, Mrs Gray." *Why is he calling?* she wondered.

"Hello, Anjou. This is Dandre'. How are you?"

"I am fine."

"Glad to hear it. I was wondering if we could meet sometime today to discuss a business proposition."

"I beg your pardon? Did you say a business proposition?"

"Yes."

The first thought that went through her mind was that engaging in business of any kind with him was not a good idea. "When would you like to meet, Dandre?"

"How about this afternoon for lunch? At the Golden Dragon?"

"OK, see you then." Andy held the phone in her hand for a while, thinking how Dandre's voice made her feel. *He sounds so ultra-sexy.* She wondered how he would sound in the thrills of passion. Dismissing all such thoughts, she turned back to her computer to continue with the blueprint.

Dandre' Neilson sat back in his chair and surveyed his surroundings. The first time he'd eaten here had been when Tyler had returned from Miami. He'd liked it then, and this would be the place he would put into motion a plan some would consider to being outrageous. They were probably right. He wasn't quite sure when he had decided over the last few weeks that Anjou Royale was destined to be his wife. Probably the first night he'd held her hand outside the restaurant when he had asked for her number. It was always the desire of Dandre's heart to fall in love with the woman of his dreams, just like his father had. The image of his mom and dad flash before his eyes. Even to this day, after being married for over thirty years, Dr Juan Neilson was still very much in love with the lovely Drusilla. The two had met while Juan was in medical school and attending the University of the West Indies in Kingston, Jamaica.

Drusilla's father, Ryan Armstrong, was the chief pathologist. It was while Drusilla was leaving her father's office after visiting him that Juan had taken one look at her, and he was a goner. The union produced four sons. His parents were loving and very affectionate, and he could see it by the way they looked at each other, the secret smiles, and the tender touches when they thought no one was watching. Dandre' could swear he has caught his mom and dad getting busy on several occasions when he had called. One time he had called, and his father had answered the phone. There was a certain sound in his voice. Dandre' had said with great concern, "Daddy, are you all right?"

His dad had replied, "Son, your mother does strange things to me that take my breath away and turn my brain to mush."

Dandre' had replied, "Dad, time out. TMI."

His father had laughed, saying "Just you wait until you find your Miss Right."

Dandre' straightened up in his seat when Andy entered the restaurant. The same feeling suffused his heart that had settled there the first night he'd seen her. God, he loved the woman. He no longer tried to rationalise why or how; it did not matter at this point. As she walked towards him, he stood. She was probably five foot seven—just the right height for his six foot three frame. He studied her expression as she got closer, and he wondered what she was thinking. *One thing is for sure: she has no idea what is about to hit her.*

"Hello, Dandre'," she greeted.

"Anjou, thank you for agreeing to see me," he said as he took her outstretched hand.

"You are welcome. It's not a problem," she said sitting in the chair he pulled out for her. "You mentioned something about meeting to discuss a business proposal?"

"That is correct, but first, how about ordering something to eat? I am famished." Dandre' summoned the maître d', who strolled over with menus and placed glasses of water on the table. "I trust you like Malaysian cuisine?"

"Are you kidding me? I am a connoisseur of food. My mom likes to cook, and I inherited that love from her."

Dandre' smiled. "In that case, what would you recommend?"

"I think you should try the ham choy and pork. It is to die for."

"What will you have?" Dandre' asked.

"I will have the mee goren."

After their order was placed, Dandre' said, "Tell me about your family."

She replied, "Well, you met my two sisters a few months ago. I have three brothers. Andre is the oldest, and he is the president of Wilson & Wilson Architecture. He is thirty-four and is married to the love of his life, Patricia. Then there is Nicholas, the second oldest. He is the director of public relations at the firm. Last but not least, Noel is a chartered accountant at Grace Kennedy & Company. He is considered to be a ladies' man."

Dandre' smiled. "I know about that too well," he said. "I have a question for you. What constitutes a man being call a ladies' man? Just because a man may enjoy the company of women, it does not necessarily make him a womaniser."

The expression on Andy's face was priceless. Dandre'

burst out laughing, and the rich sound filled the room. All heads turned in their direction.

"I know the difference between liking and enjoying female company, and being a player," she said. "So what about you, Dandre'? Do you have any siblings?"

"Yes," Dandre' replied. "When you met me a few months ago, the men who were with me are my brothers Chayse and Colar. My oldest brother was not with us; his name is Christopher."

"Do you have any sisters?"

He smile and said no. Their waiter returned with their food. The interruption by their food was a welcome respite.

Gosh! The man's aura is overwhelming, to say the least, Andy thought. She took the opportunity to study his exquisite face. He was terrifyingly beautiful. He had the kind of masculine features that a woman was prone to dream about: sensual, strong, and unyielding. In a face so arresting for its masculine perfection, it was his eyes that commanded the most attention. They were the colour of molten gold, and he had thick lashes. His wavy, bronze-gold hair was well below his shoulders and pulled back in a ponytail. His tawny golden skin was smooth as butter, and its texture was evenly sleek. As she studied him, his firm mouth moved ever so sensuously while he chewed his food. She could describe his mouth as bewitching—there were no other way to view it. There was a certain mischievous tilt to those firm, sensual, masculine, lips that gave a hint to pure pleasure. His expansive chest was athletically sculpted. His upper arms were well defined under his jacket. Simply put, the man was magnificent. Andy thought, *No man has the right to be this fine.*

Suddenly Dandre' asked, "Are you OK, Anjou?"

"Yes, I am fine." A flush covered her cheeks as she realised she was caught ogling him. After they finished eating and the waitress removed their plates, Andy leaned back in her chair and smiled at Dandre'. "Lunch was wonderful. I enjoyed every bit. Now, tell me about that business proposal."

He chuckled and reached for the folder he had placed on the chair. He handed it to her. "These are the layouts on two hundred fifty acres of land that 1 inherited. The project is twofold. I would like you to design an all-inclusive honeymoon resort with a casino, restaurants, and spa. Second I would like you to create a floor plan for my house. That will be on the second layout. That track of land is another seventy-five acres."

Andy looked up from the diagrams. "Are you serious?"

"Yes, I am. What's the matter? Are you not able to design the plans? If you are concerned about your fee, money is not an issue. I am prepared to pay 1.2 million dollars. Well, Ms Royale? What will your answer be?"

"Yes, of course I would love to design the resort and your home," Andy stammered. She lifted her eyes with a look of awe on her face. "This is prime land! I did not know you owned Duranta Repens Estate."

"It has been in my family for generations, and I would like to build my house there."

"Which project would you like me to concentrate on first?" Andy asked after she had recovered her bearings.

"The house," Dandre' said. "I plan on settling down soon in the near future."

"I see," Andy said.

"Do you?" Dandre' countered with a mysterious look in his eyes.

Andy looked, away suddenly feeling flustered and wondering why this man made her feel things she'd never felt before. Gazing into his eyes made her feel like she was drowning in a pool of liquid gold. She glanced back down at the papers in front of her. "So what exactly are your requirements? I mean, how many bedrooms and bathrooms are we talking about? This is a lot of land, and the sky is the limit with what can be done."

Dandre' chuckled at the excitement he heard in her voice. "I plan to have a boatload of children, so I will need a very large mansion."

"A boatload of children? What is it with you island men and having plenty Pinckney?"

Dandre' burst out laughing at the expression on her face. He thought to himself, *If only you knew, my lovely enchantress, that you are going to be their mother!* He sobered as she continued staring at him. "Do you not like children?" he asked, holding his breath as he waited anxiously for her answer.

"Of course I do."

"That is good to know. So, when will be a good time for me to show you the land?"

Andy reached in her handbag to retrieve her electronic notebook. She then scrolled to her calendar to check her schedule for the rest of the week. "How about the day after tomorrow?"

"Good. I will pick you up around 11.00 a.m. from your office."

"It's OK," Andy said. "I can meet you there."

"It's not a problem picking you up. There is no need for the both of us to drive if we're going to the same place."

There was nothing Andy could say to refute what Dandre' had said. After all, it did make sense for them to drive together. The only problem with that was the man had a deadly effect on her senses.

Later on that evening, Andy, Marche, and Marconnets sat in the living room of her condo sipping cocoa while she explained the business proposal Dandre' had offered her. Andy was trying her darnedest to down play the excitement she felt. From the looks on her sisters' faces and their simultaneous "Oh my goodness", she could tell that they were very happy for her.

Marche had a mischievous grin on her face as she said, "And you know what the best part about this is? Yu get to work with that hunk of a man!"

Andy rolled her eyes. "This is business. I don't have time for a summer romance with Dandre'. Besides, he may very well have a dray-load of women. I refuse to be his part-time or in-between love."

"Yeah, yeah. You need to loosen up a little, sis," Marconnets said. "Ever since things ended with you and Adam, it's almost like you died inside."

"I am very much alive, to the contrary of what the both of you think. I am just being cautious. Some men can't be trusted, and I refuse to allow myself to be taken for a ride."

"Just remember that the brave may have a short life, but the cowards never live at all," Marche said.

"I will remember that," Andy said with a smirk on her face.

"Can you promise me one thing?" Marche asked.

"What?" Andy said cautiously.

"That you will start living again?"

"What do you mean?"

"Well, you don't go anywhere. You just shut yourself off from the opposite sex. You refuse to even consider going on a date."

"Look, guys. I know you love me, and I am touched by

your concern, but don't be. I am fine, and I like my life just the way it is right now."

"I see," Marconnets said. "If you say so."

"Ms Royale, your eleven o'clock appointment has arrived."

Andy's pulse immediately kicked up a notch at her secretary's announcement. She took a deep breath and deliberately cleared her mind of everything, chiding herself, *This is nothing more than business.* "Give me a few minutes before you send him in, Mrs Gray."

After hanging up the phone, she stood and reached for her briefcase. "Dandre', please come in," she said cordially. "I will be ready to go in a few." Her hand began to shake as she shut down her computer.

"No rush," Dandre' said as his gaze floated over her while she bent over her computer. *She is so beautiful,* he thought. The woman was temptation at its best. Today, she had her hair pulled back in a ponytail, and the style emphasised the delicate column of her neck. She was wearing a dark blue suit with a pinstriped pink blouse. The outfit made her look ultra-feminine.

"Thank you, Dandre'," she said, cutting into his thoughts as she turned around. "I am ready to go." She made her way around the desk and stepped towards him.

Dandre' held the door open and stood back to allow her to proceed. As she walked by, he caught a whiff of her perfume. The light and fruity fragrance, combined with her personal scent, had a drugging and erotic effect on him. Dandre' could feel his heartbeat escalating and a certain part of his autonomy responding. Dandre' shook his head as if to clear his mind from the hypnotic state, closing the door behind him.

As they walked out to the parking lot, Dandre' said, "I thought we should visit the site for the resort first because it is the farthest."

"That's fine by me," Andy said.

Dandre' opened the front passenger door of his Jaguar to allow Andy to get in. He then closed the door and walked around to the driver's side of the vehicle. After snapping his seat belt in place, he pulled out of the parking lot and headed east towards the airport. Fifteen minutes later, they pulled into the parking lot of a private air strip.

Andy glanced at Dandre' and said, "I thought we were driving?"

With a smile on his face, Dandre' said, "No. The property is at the west end of the island, and it takes almost three hours by car. Why drive when it only takes forty minutes by air? Besides, as the owner of Triple X Aviation, I do have aircraft at my disposal."

Andy was momentarily at a loss for words. She had no idea that Dandre' owned the blasted company—she simply thought he worked there.

By the look on her face, Dandre' could tell that she had no idea that he was one of the wealthiest men in Negril. He smiled inwardly.

Just then, a uniformed chauffer stepped to the car as Dandre' pulled into the parking space reserved for him. Andy stepped from the car suddenly feeling lightheaded as she viewed her surroundings. The place was bussing with activities. There were aircraft mechanics, pilots, and stewardesses, as well as passengers rushing through the revolving doors to make their scheduled flights. "I take it this is your private airstrip?" Andy asked.

"Yes," Dandre' replied. "After building my first fleet of planes, I had this airstrip built in the interim. It was cheaper to own my own than to lease or rent one. Operating a business such as this can be very expensive."

"So, what king of service do you offer?" she asked.

Chuckling, Dandre' said, "From building aircraft to providing charter services. You name it, and we'll deliver. Triple X Aviation takes the guesswork out of aircraft management and flying for our private and corporate clients. We have established relationships with all foreign and domestic flight operators in the world and in our network. Each private air charter operator's specialty dictates what we can offer our clients. We provide a home base that will generate the most revenue on your jet or aircraft, regardless of its type and size. We also market your aircraft to our private charter market, and we customise an aircraft management program to your requirements. Triple X offsets the cost of owning a plane. You retain full control of your executive jet, and we generate additional revenue by optimizing empty legs. It's a floating fleet for one-way charters. Keep your aircraft moving when you are not. We also specialise in sophisticated solutions to mission-critical projects."

"Wow," Andy said. "There is a lot to that."

Dandre' replied, "Flying isn't a challenge when you're an expert. By delivering integrated and innovative aviation solutions, we take care of both the big plans and minute details, tailoring every aspect of air travel to your exacting needs. Our approach combines the exclusivity of your own jet with the flexibility of an entire fleet. The global aviation marketplace is filled with many options and solutions. You see, what works for one client isn't necessarily right for another. Our company offers a unique consultancy approach, using over a decade of experience to handcraft individualised solutions for every client. It's a method that consistently delivers choice and value for wide ranges of global clients. With that approach we have a 92 per cent return on clients."

CHAPTER 3

To the left of Andy were several aircraft of varying sizes, all with the Jamaican National Bird logo displaying the words "Piece of Jamaica That Flies." Dandre' placed his hand on her elbow as he gently guided her to an aircraft that was already sitting on the runway.

Aboard the BXL360 craft, the steward said, "Welcome aboard, Mr Neilson. It's a pleasure to have you flying with us today."

"Thanks, Sandi," Dandre' said. "It's good to be here." He led Andy towards the middle of the aircraft and motioned for her to take a seat. Andy chose a window seat on the right side of the craft, and Dandre' chose the seat facing her. The steward indicated to Andy to fasten her seat belt as Dandre' headed for the cockpit to have a word with the pilot.

Andy could still feel the imprint of Dandre' fingers on her elbow. She was annoyed with herself for allowing him to affect her to the extent that he did. The inside of the craft, though small, spoke of luxury. She could tell that this was not the corporate jet. She mused to herself, *If this is so elegantly decorated in burgundy and grey with plush seats, what does the corporate jet look and feel like?*

Andy was brought out of her reverie as the pilot's voice came over the intercom. "Welcome aboard the BXL360, ladies and gentlemen. Please fasten your seat belts, sit back, relax, and enjoy your flight. We will be cruising at an altitude of thirty thousand feet." Andy pressed her lips firmly together as she looked at the man sitting across from her. She thought the same thing now as she had the night she'd met him at Sunset Negril. *He is the most beautiful man that I have ever laid eyes on.* That was why she was more determined than ever to keep up her guard. The last thing she needed was a man, especially one who was as fine as Dandre'. *Still …* Although she tried not to stare, she could not help being drawn to him. If she was honest with herself, she was hopelessly attracted to him—and that was not a good sign.

She was wondering whether she had made the right decision in accepting the job when Dandre' said, "Penny for your thoughts?"

Her cheeks flushed as she realised that she was caught staring at him again. She quickly glanced out the window before saying, "Nothing you would be interested in."

"Try me," said Dandre'.

She cleared her throat and said, "Tell me about Duranta Repens Estate."

A slight smile played at his lips. He knew exactly what she was trying to do. *So she is trying to keep it professional. Well, that's fine by me. I will give her that, because in the next few weeks I intend to get mine. Sooner rather than later, she will know that Dandre' plays for keeps and keeps what belongs to him.*

He said, "Westmoreland is the western-most parish in Jamaica, located on the south of downtown. It's the southern portion of the so-called Seven Miles Beach. When the road between Montego Bay and Negril was improved in the early 1970s, it helped increase Negril's status as a new resort location. It was a two-lane paved road that ran approximately a hundred yards inland from two white coral beaches, at the southern end of which was a small village. The long, paved road from the village ran north to Green Island, home to many workers in Negril. It was then that my grandparents decided to build a private airstrip, Negril Aerodrome. It was built in the mid-seventies near Rutland Points, catering to North American and European winter tourists."

Andy was so engrossed in what Dandre' was saying that she thought she could listen to the sound of his voice forever. The rich timbre flowed over her like the caress of a gentle summer breeze.

Eventually, the voice of the pilot came over the intercom as the plain prepared for its final descent. The flight attendant came to collect the glass and debris from their refreshment. The plane taxied down the runway to the gate, and Andy saw a sleek black limo waiting to take them to his estate.

As the car pulled up to the entrance of the property, Andy realised she was holding her breath. The scene before her was breathtaking, and the beautiful lush shrubs and foliage was a sight to behold. The car came to a stop, and the chauffeur opened the door. Andy exclaimed, "Oh my. This is beautiful!"

As they strolled through the dirt road, they could smell the fresh saltwater from the sea. There were all kinds of fruit trees: mango, nesberry, pineapple, grapefruit, coconut, plum, cherry, and banana. The sound of the sea could be heard from a distance. As they travelled further inland, Andy could see that this was a very high-potential oceanfront property, with four acres of seafront and ten acres on the other side of walkway. Between the walkway and sandy cliffs was sandy ground to create a beach. There were retaining walls to the seafront, already built.

Andy turned to Dandre' and said, "This is the perfect place for the development."

"I agree," Dandre' said as he took her hand. "Come with me. I would like to show you something." He led her to the east side of the property. Dandre' came to a stop. In front of some low-hanging vines was a waterfall settling in a pool at the base of a little hill. He said, "This is a natural mineral bath that I would like to be incorporated in the health spa that you will design. The water is naturally hot, about 120 degrees."

Andy stooped down and placed her hand in the hot water, which had a soothing effect. "Gosh, this water feels so good. I wish I could get in it." She straightened up, turned around, and collided with Dandre's massive chest. He immediately placed his arms around her to keep her from falling.

"Anjou …" His mouth was mere centimetres from hers. She could feel his moist breath on her lips as he moaned her name. She could not answer, and as if on their own accord, her lips inched closer to his. Desires of the most potent kind sliced through her, which causes shivers to dance up and down her spine. He captured her in his hypnotic gaze, and she could not seem to look away. Those golden, sensual depths became her universe. She found herself looking into his soul. There was a wildness to him that would never be controlled; he was feral at heart.

His mouth descended firmly to claim hers. His velvet lips parted slightly as he captured hers—a taking that seared her with raw passion. He tasted of the untamed. He inhaled her rapid exhalation deep into his lungs as if he were taking her very life into himself. Andy blinked, and she could not breathe. The trees around her began to spin; she felt faint. She frantically struggled with a surge of force. He breathed back into her mouth, giving her breath back to her, which was now mingled with his breath of sugar and Konica spice. She greedily inhaled this rush of warm air, clinging to his ravishing lips. At her action, he groaned deeply into her mouth as he captured her tongue. He lifted his lips from hers, capturing her bottom lip between his teeth, which he then released gradually as he used his tongue to give her mouth one last sensuous lick before he stepped back and released his hold on her.

For a long moment, Andy could not look at Dandre'. It took her a while to get her bearings back, and when she did, she began talking about the building plan and where the different section of the building would go. Dandre' knew she was rambling because she was embarrassed. *Good,* he thought. She was deeply affected by his kiss. He smiled inwardly. At least she did not try to slap his face. This was the beginning of levels of pleasure to which he intended to introduce her.

Back in the car, Andy closed her eyes. She had never behaved inappropriately with a client before, and she wasn't sure what had brought it on today. What a sensual person she turned out to be! Andy watched, bemused, as Dandre' sat across from her. A kiss and a touch, and she went up in flames. Why had she not recognised her true nature before? How could she have been disdainful to other women who succumbed to the all-too-potent allure of desire? She had never felt it before until now. If it had not been for this trip today with Dandre', she might have missed this wild elation that still simmered in her blood. She chalked it up to a weak moment when she yielded to temptation. She must be on her guard against it from now on. Not that she thought Dandre' would pick up from where they had left off. It was best if nothing similar happened again, especially because they would be working together.

Or was it? What if no man ever made her feel this way again? What if this is the only opportunity that she would have to experience true fulfilment?

Over the next couple of days, Andy and Dandre' dialogued over the phone as they discussed the floor plan for his house, including number of bedrooms and bathrooms, and the kitchen. Not once had he mentioned their kiss. The thought that he could ignore the kiss they had shared irritated her. It seemed she was the only one who was consumed with the memory of how he tasted but and smelled. Even though it'd been days, her nostrils still flared from that elusive scent of his. The taste of him was deeply embedded in her taste buds. Her disappointment and irritation didn't make any sense.

Andy grew restless with her thoughts and decided it was time to call it a day. She turned off her computer and headed for the door.

"Dandre', are you listening? Did you hear a word" Chayse asked. "What's wrong with him?"

"Do you remember Roger Blake?" Tyler asked.

"Yes, the goalkeeper that played for St Jago College."

"The one and the same. He died of a brain aneurysm this morning. His father is one of Dandre's partners, I know."

"Wow, I am so sorry to hear. He was so young and had a very promising future."

"Yeah. Parents are not supposed to bury their children; it's supposed to be the other way around. Why do bad things happen to good people?" Colar asked.

"Don't think any of us have the answer to that. You will have to ask the Almighty when you see Him," Christopher said with a smile.

Dandre' spoke for the first time. "OK, guys. On a lighter

note, who is ready to play dominos? There is jerk chicken and Red Stripe beer, so you can help yourselves."

"Sure. You up for the challenge, Dandre'?" Colar said. "Because if your money's burning holes in your pocket, I am prepared to drop a couple six love on you and take it all."

"Man, you always talking smack," Tyler said. "I recall the last time we played, you lost three Gs, bro."

"Crap. Why you have to bring that up? You just like to rain on a brother's parade?"

"Yeah, little brother. You like running your mouth, so we've got to keep you in check," Christopher said, laughing.

"So tell me, Colar Did you get Paige's number yet?" Chayse asked.

"Nah," Colar replied.

"Say what? Don't whisper. The last time we were at the restaurant, you bragged how you were going to get her number before the night was over."

"I never had a chance. Remember that before I could make my move, they left, and brother dearest went chasing after them."

"That has never stopped you before," Chayse said. "Are you losing your touch?"

"Who is Paige?" Christopher and Tyler asked.

"Oh, it's this smoking-hot redhead who was at the Sunset Negril. She was hanging with her friends. Man, she was fine. To be truthful, all of them were fine. I think ever since, Colar has been having wet dreams about her." All eyes were on Colar as they laughed at him.

"You all aren't right," he said. "But I *will* get her number. As a matter of fact, I think I will do one better than that. I will take her to the governor's ball as my date."

"Yeah, right," Christopher said with mockery in his voice.

He winked at the others. If anything could get their little brother going, it was a dare.

"Maybe you all should ask Dandre' about his lady love …"

"Yes, and who is that?" asked Christopher.

"Oh, you don't know? Well, let me enlighten you," Colar said with a grin. "Her name is Anjou Royale. I think big bro is in love. She is drafting the designs for the resort and his house."

"Is that so, Dandre'?" Christopher asked.

"Yes, it is so," Dandre' said. "Now, whose play is it?"

"Wait just a minute. I am lost," Chayse said.

"Where are you lost?"

"Between the designs and being in love. Are you saying you are in love, Dandre'?" Chayse asked. All eyes were on Dandre' as they waited for his answer.

"What if I am? What is that to you?" he said.

The room got deadly quite as they stared at him with shock written all over their faces. "Wow. To capture your heart, my brother, she must be a very special lady," Christopher finally said.

Dandre' parked his car behind Andy's SUV in her driveway. He stepped on the veranda, and as he rang the doorbell, his heart was beating a mile per minute. He wondered for the millionth time whether he was going to have a heart attack. No woman had ever affected him the way Anjou did. He felt like a teenager going on his first date as he waited for Andy to open the door.

After stepping out of the bathtub, Andy reached for the bath towel to wrap around her. She wondered which one of her sisters had forgotten her keys again and needed to be let in. As she headed for the front door, she thought, *Why give a key if my sisters don't use it?* Without checking to see who it was, she opened the door. "Dandre'! What are you doing here?"

"Hello, Anjou. May I come in?" For a moment she could say nothing and stood staring at him. "May I come in?" he asked again.

Andy licked her lips, which had suddenly gone dry, before stepping back and saying, "Sure." Andy closed the door and leaned against it for support, feeling weak at the knees. She was afraid that she would fall. "What are you doing here, Dandre'?"

Dandre' looked at her and could see surprise written on her face. "Come dancing with me tonight," he said in a sexy, lazy drawl.

"Dancing? I don't think that's a good idea," Andy said, looking into the golden depths of his eyes. She did not realise he had moved. *The man has the gait of a Panther, light and graceful.* She could feel his warm breath on her face.

"That's not the right answer for a beautiful and desirable woman wrapped in a bath towel, to say to a man who is dangerously attracted to her," Dandre' said as he gently licked his lips. "We could have our own private party here, and I happen to like dirty dancing," he added with a chuckle.

Andy tried to push Dandre' away, and her movement caused the towel to come undone and slip to the floor. Glancing down, Dandre' eyes collided with the most perfect pair of breasts he had ever seen. He groaned deep in his throat, bent his head, and took one of caramel globes in his hot mouth.

At the impact of Dandre's lips on her breast, Andy cried out in pleasure. Dandre' began to suck and lick her breast. Andy grabbed his head to keep his mouth in position.

Dandre' slowly caressed her abdomen, and her skin felt just like he knew it would: soft, smooth, and supple. He slowly moved his hands lower until he reached the mass of curly hair at the apex of her legs. He felt her shudder from his touch and decided to take things further. Using his fingers, he found what he was looking for. She was hot and wet, and he began to stroke her flower, the part of her that would give her intense pleasure. Dandre', the master of seduction, lift his head from her breast as he captured her mouth in a sensual, hot kiss. His finger entered her, and she began to shudder and tremble as waves of sensation surged through her. Then there was the purring sound she was making deep in her throat; it was driving him insane.

He lifted his head as he began to whisper, "Venu pour moi, mon amour … Come for me, my love." He drove her over the edge and felt her knees weaken. He held her up as he continued to stroke her inside.

Andy screamed in his mouth as wave after wave of pleasure surged through her body. An orgasm rocked her body, shaking her to the core. Andy wrapped her arms around Dandre's neck and buried her face in his chest as she tried to gasp for air.

Dandre' picked her up in his arms and walked to the centre of the room. "Where is your bedroom?" he asked. He breathed deeply as he inhaled the essence of her womanly fragrance. Following her direction, he pushed the bedroom door open and gently laid Andy on the bed. He then brought his hands to his mouth and licked the fingers he'd used to pleasure her a few moments ago. Dandre' bent over Andy and said, "You take my breath away. I think I should leave while I am still in control." With that, he walked out the door.

Andy lay on the bed where Dandre' had placed her. She

tried to wrap her mind around what had just happened at her front door. How could a man give her an orgasm with a kiss and a couple of his fingers? She mused as she drifted off to sleep.

No woman had ever affected Dandre' the way Anjou did. Even now, the alluring, potent smell of her still clung to him, and he had a gigantic erection that he was afraid would break his zipper at any minute. He closed his eyes as he remembered those erotic purring sounds she'd made while she surrendered to the ministration of his fingers. He almost lost it as she came apart in his arms, and he knew they would be good together in bed even though he did not go all the way. As inexperience as she was, she had touched something deep inside him that no other woman had. God, the woman was so sensual that he can't wait to explore all the untapped passion she possessed. Dandre' knew something had to give. He had to win Anjou's heart. She consumed his thoughts during the day, and at nights she became the woman of his wet dreams. Being in an aroused state was very uncomfortable and embarrassing, to say the least.

It was Saturday night, and Dandre' was at home nursing a glass of scotch on the rocks and a hard-on. He had every intention of taking Anjou to the dance tonight, but when she opened the door wrapped in a bath towel, he became unglued. Pacing the floor in his home, Dandre' exhaled a frustrated breath. He picked up the phone to call his friend Tyler, but he remembered that he was out of the country. After replacing the receiver, he muttered a string of colourful words in French that would make a sailor look like a saint. He headed for the bedroom, stripped off his clothes, and stepped in the bathroom to take a very cold shower. Not that it matter anyway. There were women who would give anything and everything to spend one minute in his company. Yet the one woman whom he desired and wanted to be with acted as if she was going to the gallows every time he requested her presence. It was ridiculous. He desperately needed to gain some control over his emotions.

Later, Dandre' was sitting across the table from Christopher. This was just what he needed: some time with his brother to unwind.

"By the way," Christopher began as they waited for their drinks to be served, "Mommy came to see me this afternoon, and she informed Melody it's time you get married and give her a grandchild. So be warned. I believe she is on a quest to find you a wife if you don't present a future daughter-in-law soon."

Dandre' groaned inwardly. "Don't remind me. Please tell me you and our mother were not discussing my sex life, or the lack thereof."

"Hey, don't shoot the messenger. Mommy brought it up."

"Damn. I am a dead man," Dandre' wailed as he buried his face in his hands.

Christopher's hoot of laughter echoed throughout the room, causing several curious glances to be directed their way.

"You are enjoying my dilemma, aren't you?"

"To be quite honest, yes, I am," Christopher replied with a huge grin on his face. "Consider it payback for the hell you gave me when I was trying to win Melody's heart."

"Hey, I was just trying to protect my big brother from heartbreak," Dandre' said as he joined in the laughter.

"Mommy just wants you to be happy, Dandre'. We all do."

"I am happy, and I will deal with my relationship in my own way. I don't need Mom to find me a woman."

"But you both want the same thing."

"Yeah, but I can't let her know that I want what she wants. Neither will I give in to her every whim."

Christopher stared at his brother in exasperation. After throwing his hand in the air, he exclaimed, "You are hopeless!"

"Yeah, yeah. So I have been told before," Dandre' said.

"How are things going with Andy?"

"I have invited her out several times, but each time she gracefully declines. I am not giving up so quickly. I have a master plan that will sweep Anjou off her feet."

"Let's drink to your master plan."

"From what I understand, she is really afraid of getting involved. The last relationship ended badly, leaving her with a broken heart."

"Do you think she is over her ex?" Christopher asked.

"Yes, she is, but she swore she would never give her heart to another man."

"Then you have your work cut out for you. But I have confidence in you. I am sure you will be able to convince her. You are a Neilson, and we never give up on anything we set our hearts to achieve."

"You are right about that," Dandre' said, chuckling as he sipped his drink. "By the way, do you and Melody know what you are having?"

"No," Christopher replied. "Melody wants this to be a surprise. She is decorating the nursery in green and white. That way if we have a boy, the colours are still applicable."

"Good choice. What about names? Have you decided on those yet?"

"Yeah. If we have a boy, we will name him Adrian, after her late brother. If she has a girl, we will call her Rachel."

"Sounds like you guys have it all figured out. I am happy for you."

"Thank you, my brother," Christopher said. "Next month, I think will be a baby shower. I know your presence is required."

"I don't think that will be a problem. I can see Colar whining about being there." Dandre' chuckled.

CHAPTER 4

Andy arrived at the office an hour earlier than usual because she wanted to complete a design she had started the previous weekend. As she sat facing her computer screen, she allowed her mind to reflect on what had happened at her home Saturday night. No man had ever made her feel that way. Neither had any man come close to making her forget everything except being in his arms with his mouth on hers. *Would I be so terrible to sleep with him? It need only be once to satisfy this painful longing, to see what it would be like as the centre and focus of so much passion and power.*

It was unlikely to go beyond that, she was sure. He had so many duties and responsibilities—too many for any affair of any length of time. Marriage would never cross Dandre's mind. If and when he sought a wife, it would be someone who moved in his exalted circle, a polished and sophisticated woman of equal lineage, equal wealth. Boy, was she in trouble. Her body kept reminding her of what Dandre's hands and lips had given her. Truthfully, she had slept like a baby. To say the least, she had enjoyed every stroke, every touch, and every kiss he had given her.

There was one thing that bothered her. Why didn't he seek his own pleasure when he took her to bedroom? Was it because he knew she was inexperienced? Was he turned off by it? It must be true about the rumours she'd heard. Men only desired experienced and sophisticated women in their beds. To cross that line into the passion and ecstasy of moment seemed possible, but to court it deliberately was something else. She was not impulsive and seldom acted without good and sufficient reason. A vagrant desire was not enough to make her tear off her clothes and throw herself at Dandre' Neilson. She would have to be sure before she took the final step.

After shaking her head in disgust, Andy picked up her pencil and began sketching. Sometime later, the door to Andy's office bust open, and Gail walked in with a beautiful basket and the most gorgeous bouquet of flowers. "Hi there," she said as she placed the items on Andy's desk.

"Hello," Andy replied as she pushed her chair back and walk towards her friend. "Where are you coming from, and who gave you gifts?" she asked Gail.

"These are not mine—they are yours. I was on my way to see you when the courier brought them to Mrs Gray. I told her I would bring them to you. Come on. Unwrap the basket. I want to see what's in it. And there is also a card with the bouquet."

With trembling hands, Andy unwrapped the basket to reveal a large red box with her name written in silver letters. She removed the bow and lifted the lid to reveal an assortment of French chocolate from La Maison du Chocolate.

"Oh my. These are my favourite! Fruited French chocolate Palmira—a coconut praline. The chocolate gives back its notable flavour to crunchy hazelnuts, coconut, and caramelised cocoa nibs. Then there is Jolika: almond paste–flavoured slivers of pistachio are scattered throughout the chocolate. Finally, there is Salvador: ganache with fresh raspberry pulp under a dark chocolate couverture." Andy was speechless. "Who in the world would send these?" She reached for the envelope and quickly opened the message.

"Tu es mon coeur—you are my heart. Dandre'."

A lump formed in Andy's throat. How did Dandre' know she liked French chocolate and purple roses?

Gail said, "Well, who is this mystery man?"

Andy replied, "Dandre'."

"Wow. He sent you these all the way from Paris? I am impressed. This man intends to sweep you off your feet and is doing a hell of a job."

Andy replied, "You like him?" Just then, Andy's private line rang. "Hello?" she said.

"Anjou, it's Dandre'. Did you receive the bouquet and basket I sent you?"

"Yes, thank you. They are beautiful. You didn't have to send me anything."

"I wanted to, Anjou," Dandre' said in a husky voice. "I will be back tomorrow, and I want you to go to the opera with me."

"We don't have an opera house in Negril."

"I know. It's in New York. Be ready at 3.30. I will pick you up."

"Fine. See you then. Goodbye." Andy hung up the phone. Her heart was beating so fast, and there were shivers dancing up and down her spine.

"So you are going to New York? How exciting! I am happy for you. What will you wear?" Gail asked.

"I don't know. I guess we should go shopping."

Dandre' arrived at exactly 3.30. Before he could ring the doorbell, Andy opened the door. Dandre's breath caught in his throat at he stared at her. "Hello, Anjou. You look beautiful. May I come in?"

"Yes," she said as she stepped back to allow him to enter.

Dandre' closed the door behind him. He had this insatiable desire to take her in his arms and kiss her until she purred like a satisfied cat. He missed her taste, her sent, and everything about her. But he didn't think she would appreciate him touching her. He reached in his coat pocket and pulled out a long, flat box. He opened it and said, "I wanted you to have this."

Andy gave an audible gasp as she looked at the diamond necklace nestled on a bed of black velvet.

"Here. Turn around and let me clasp the closure for you."

"It is beautiful," Andy said. "I don't know if I can accept such an expensive gift."

"Nonsense," he said as he looked at her with satisfaction. She slowly turned around to face him. "Are you ready? Let's go."

A shudder gripped her, shaking her to her toes at the tone of his voice and the look in his eyes.

Andy placed her hand at her throat. Tears streamed from her eyes as she watched the final act of the opera. She was enamoured with the story of two people who were in love but were torn apart because of their social and economic backgrounds. Dandre' gently placed a handkerchief in her hand. He was moved by her sensitivity and watched her wipe away her tears as the final curtain came down.

So this is the famous Metropolitan Opera House, Andy thought as she stared up at the beautiful chandelier. They we sitting in the balcony, and their seats almost hung over the stage. It was situated at the western end of Lincoln Center Plaza. The Metropolitan Opera faced Columbus Avenue and Broadway, and it formed an axis with Philip Johnson's David Koch Theater, with the plaza fountain at its centre. The building was clad in white travertine, and the east façade was graced with its distinctive series of five concrete arches with large glass and bronze. It towered ninety-six feet above the plaza. On the north, south, and west sides of the building, hundreds of vertical fins of travertine running the full height of the structure gave the impression that the façade was an uninterrupted mass of travertine when viewed from certain angles. The building totalled fourteen stories, five of which were underground.

The opera house had a modernist genre and had a seating capacity of 3,800. On display in the lobby, and visible to the outside plaza, were two murals created for the space. They were approximately thirty feet high. The south walls held the work entitled *The Triumph of Music*. The north wall contained *The Source of Music*. The multi-story lobby was dominated by a concrete and terrazzo cantilevered stairway that connected the main level with the lower level lounges and upper floors. The centrepiece of the lobby was an array of eleven crystal chandeliers resembling constellations with sparkly moons and satellites spraying out in all directions. The auditorium contained twenty-one large, beautiful chandeliers. It was an exquisite and spectacular sight to behold; she had never seen anything quite like it.

They sat in their seats for a while as they waited for the other guests to exit. Dandre' leaned towards Andy and asked, "Did you enjoy the performance, mon cheri?"

"Yes, I did," she replied with a smile. "It is kind of sad thought that our hero had to walk away from the love of his life."

"You are right. It is sad that he had to walk away," he

said as he gently took her hand in his. "Are you ready? Shall we go?"

"Yes, I am ready," she said as she got to her feet.

Andy didn't drink except on rare occasions, but tonight she felt an exception. She accepted the glass of sherry the flight attendant handed her as she sat beside Dandre' on his plane. To say the least, the aircraft spoke of luxury and opulence. Dandre's nearness was wreaking havoc with her senses. *He smells so good. Oh God.* She had an intense desire to taste him all over. Where did those thoughts come from? To be honest, ever since that Saturday night eight weeks ago, when he had kissed her into an orgasm, she wanted more. Her body seemed to be on fire not just for any man, but one particular man with golden eyes. Andy began to squirm in her seat as liquid heat gathered between her legs.

"Are you OK?" Dandre's deep voice rumbled in her ear.

Andy opened her mouth to answer him, but no sound came. Suddenly she felt hot all over.

Dandre' leaned over and captured her mouth with his, kissing her thoroughly. He licked her lips, and she tingled all over. "Mmm," she muttered.

He slipped his tongue inside her mouth. Andy sighed into his plundering mouth, and Dandre' purred louder, taking the offering of her breath. He inhaled it, and his strong finger began to slide through her hair as he gently massaged her scalp. "Tell me," he coaxed her, "that you want me." His tongue slid against hers in a measured, languorous stroke.

Andy shivered, and a groan came from her throat. He withdrew his tongue to nip delicately at the edge of her lips with his teeth. Then he captured her upper lip between his own and suckled on it. Andy began to quiver at the incredible sensations.

"Tell me, that you want me …" he repeated.

She had no idea what was happening to her. She gasped for breath and mumbled in a voice that did not sound like her own. "I want you, Dandre'. Please make love to me."

Dandre' used his hand to gently caress her neck and throat as he muttered, "Very well, my seductress. Your wish is my command. I shall grant you every desire of your heart."

He slipped within her mouth once more. She rhythmically surge inside, and her entire body began to throb. Andy was not aware she was making purring sounds of pleasure, so caught up was she in his feral hot passion as he built sensation after sensation. Her body was throbbing to the wild rhythm he was giving.

Dandre' opened his mouth and used his tongue to make an erotic circular motion as he purred deeply in her mouth. A powerful vibration flew through her as he prolonged the low, exciting sound. Andy screamed at the exquisite, pulsating sensation flowed through her body. Dandre' swallowed her cries of ecstasy as she sagged against him and tried to catch her breath.

"You will stay with me tonight, mon amour. This is a foretaste of what is to come," he said in a sexy, husky voice.

Dandre's car was parked at the airport. When they exited the aircraft, he took her hand in his and led her to the waiting car. When she was seated with her seat belt fastened, he closed the door and walked to the driver's side. As he pulled away, he said, "Go ahead and take a nap. I will wake you when we are home." Taking his advice, Andy closed her eyes as the gentle motion of the car lulled her to sleep.

"Wake up, Anjou. We are here."

She slowly opened her eyes and glanced out the window at her surroundings.

"Would you like something to drink?" Dandre' asked.

"If you don't mind, I would like to take a bath first."

"No problem. You can use the Jacuzzi or the bath in the master suite."

Later that night, as Andy lay in the huge bed, Dandre' nuzzled his chin against her shoulder. He began to shower her shoulder blade with butterfly kisses as he worked his way down her back. With his skilled mouth on her, he caused her to lose every though in her head except the feel of him. Dandre' liked the taste of her, and he kissed her deeply and passionately. He sucked on her tongue, exploring the inner recesses of her mouth and nibbling at her lips as if it was a delicate treat. Andy kissed him back, enjoying his expertise in the simple act. She remembered how he had opened his sensual mouth over hers to purr in her mouth on the plane, and she wondered if he was going to use the same technique to bring her to an orgasm again.

Dandre' had no intention of giving her an orgasm by kissing her, as he had the last time. As he continued to kiss and nip at her lips, he used his hands to cup her breasts and gently tease her nipples. Andy groaned deep in her throat. His strong fingers threaded through her long hair, letting the silken strands sift gradually through his fingers as he examined the silken sheen.

He used the back of his hand to brush against the caramel skin of her collarbone in a feathery caress. His gifted mouth promised her nothing but pure pleasure. Andy clung to his sensuous lips and arched her back as male fingers whispered a sensitizing pattern down her breasts. Dandre' kissed his way across her chest and used his tongue to create a stimulating path as he captured one breast in his hot mouth. He then repeated the ministrations to the other breast. He used his tongue to lick his way to her abdomen as he stopped to pay homage to her navel.

Dandre' gently blew his warm breath on her stomach, which sent delicious shivers all over her. He nibbled the rounded curve of her belly, and his palm rubbed the length of her thigh and calf. He worked his way to her delicate ankle, and he kissed his way to her toes as he captured them in his mouth. Using his hand, he gently nudge her legs apart as he caressed the inner part of her legs and moved towards the apex of her thighs.

Andy thought she would die from the sheer pleasure. His hand was between her legs as his finger began to stroke her sex. Then he bent his head as he replaced his fingers with his mouth. She cried out his name and drew in a deep breath. She'd never been kissed like this before. Her mind went blank of all conscious thought, except for him and what he was doing to her. She felt pleasure of the most intense kind, deep and profound and all the way to her bones.

She purred aloud when he deepened the kiss. His tongue was just as wicked as his hands and lips. Sensation beyond belief overwhelmed her, and she groaned deep within her throat as the first wave of ecstasy washed over her. She held his head in place as his tongue increased its strokes and tasted her hungrily. Tremor after tremor rocked her body. After moving upon her once again, he covered her mouth in a fiery possession as he kissed her senseless. He whispered in her ears, "Je veux être à l'interieur de vous … I want to be inside you." He rubbed his engorged shaft against the delicate folds of her femininity. Andy moaned at the thick surge between her legs. Dandre' slid back and forth along her inner lips as he whispered naughty and erotic things to her in French. His tongue stroked hers, and she moaned against him, caught up in his spell. He rotated his hips against her, the head of his shaft pressing against her dewy moisture. Whimpering sounds of desire escape her lips as she opened her thighs for him. Andy thrashed in the intimate embrace as his hand encircled her hips. She wanted him with an intensity she never knew existed between a man and a woman.

She moaned against his lips, begging him to appease this longing he had created. Then she felt the tip of his big shaft as he entered her. Andy was tight and wet as he slid into her.

A surge of pleasure went through him from the crown of his head to the sole of his feet as he buried himself deep in her body. He saw the quick moment of pain flash across her face as he broke through the barrier. "Dandre'!" she screamed. He groaned a feral response before nipping her shoulder. His silken lips sipped at her jawline, and then he let his mouth brush tantalizingly against her nose. A low moan of satisfaction hummed from him. He was conscious of her untried state and moved carefully within her, using long, slow thrusts designed to acclimate her to him.

The even rocking motion built and built until Andy thought she could take no more. "Oh my God. What are you doing to me?" she panted. Surely nothing could be more pleasurable as she wrapped her legs around his waist. Dandre', the master of seduction, held nothing back. He thrust into her with a steady rhythm that made Andy tremble from head to toe as wild pleasure built between her legs. He gave her more pleasure each stroke. Each trust was designed to shatter her. She reared up as rapid explosion surged through her, and she screamed his name as she let herself go.

"Me regarder, mon amoureux … Look at me, sweetheart," Dandre' said. She opened her eyes and did as he asked. She met his gaze as her body came apart, and she watched as his own body stiffened while waves of pleasure surge through him. He increased the pace of their rhythm as he threw his head back and whispered, "Je t'aime … I love you."

It was a perfect release of their first union as he released his seed in her. He sagged against her before lifting himself to his elbows to stare down at her. Andy gazed up at him in awe, gasping for breath. After tossing back his silken hair, he gave her a sexy grin before kissing her on her lips.

The next morning Andy woke to the smell of freshly squeezed orange juice, french toast, scrambled eggs, bacon, and coffee. "Good morning, sleepyhead," Dandre' said in a lazy, sexy drawl. He was standing at the foot of the bed with a tray in his hand.

"Good morning," she said shyly, colour staining her cheeks as she recalled the activities of last night. "Why didn't you wake me?"

"Well, I knew you were tired. Besides, I wanted to serve you breakfast in bed."

"Oh." *Damn. He's an exquisite lover as well as being sensitive and considerate,* Andy thought. *I could get used to this.*

"So, are you ready to eat?" Before she could answer, her stomach gave a loud rumble. "I guess that answers it!" Dandre' laughed as he walk towards her. He sat at the foot of the bed and watched Andy eat. His heart did a million somersaults in his chest. Now he understood what his father had said some time ago: desire flowed through him like a hot lava. He desired her deeply. It was getting stronger with every passing moment. Even though he expected it to happen after what they had shared last night and into the early hours of the morning, he was nonetheless surprised by the depth of his desire for her. Suddenly he has this intense desire to reveal himself to her, to share all the things he kept hidden. In time, he would open up to her; somehow he knew he could trust her with his heart. Last night he had told her he loved her in French. He knew she did not understand what he'd said. For now, he would refrain from telling her in English. If he proposed to her now, would she accept or run away? A fierce battle raged within him. He knew she was the one for him. Fearing he would scare her off, Dandre' decided to hold his peace and take it one day at a time. He was thankful that she was here with him in his bed, which was more than he could ever dream of. He desperately wanted to restore her trust; after all, it was a foolish and selfish person who would have deliberately hurt another human being by betraying her trust.

Dandre' knew only too well what if felt like to have one's trust dashed to pieces. He himself had experienced such betrayal. The unpleasant memories of his last fight with Wendy three years ago surfaced. They were in London, and he had gone to the jeweller to have them customise a pearl necklace for her. That was when he had seen her with her other lover. The bitterness that rose up in him was corrosive. He remembered saying, "Why did you go there, Wendy? Or can I guess? Was the temptation to see Mullings too great for you to resist? Did you want to see what effect you would have on him? Why did you allow him to take you to his house and make love to you? Oh, let me guess: his bank account is much larger than mine."

She stared at him for a moment. It was obvious that she was caught red-handed; lying would do no good. So she flung hateful words. "Yes, he can give me much more than you ever could, so you don't deny it."

He was watching her with menacing intensity, the rage so

clearly discernible in the depth of his golden eyes, igniting a strange mixture of misery and triumph inside.

She continued. "Why should I deny that he is far wealthier and has more experience in the ways of the world than you? Furthermore, I want to be free to enjoy a sexual relationship with someone else other than you."

"If it's sex you want, then I can satisfy that need for you here and now."

Too late Wendy realised her mistake, and she made a hasty retreat through the door. The box containing the necklace fell to the floor with a thud.

Dandre' knew in his heart that Anjou was not like Wendy. In fact, she was unlike any other woman he had met.

Andy felt Dandre' scrutiny and looked up. "Why are you staring at me like that?" she asked.

"How am I looking at you?" he countered.

"Never mind. This breakfast is delicious. Did you prepare it?"

"Yes," Dandre' said with a sheepish grin on his face. "I do know my way around the kitchen. Mommy made sure my brothers and I learned how to cook."

'You were a good student," Andy said as she licked her fingers.

Dandre' rose from where he was sitting and walk towards Andy. He leaned forward and gave her mouth a sensuous lick to capture the jelly that was on her lips.

Andy tingled all over as images of last night flashed before her eyes. She reached up and captured his head as she latched on to his mouth. Dandre' growled deep in his throat as he returned her kiss. Andy wrapped her arms around his neck, enjoying the kiss. She opened her mouth, and he inserted his tongue, taking full advantage of what she was offering him.

Andy removed her hand from around his neck and began to stroke his hair. Dandre' purred like a contented cat. What she did not know was that he liked to be touched like that; it was one of his erogenous zones. The more she stroked his hair, the harder he got. He kissed her with sexual savagery that shocked her, and yet beneath that there were threads of such pure pleasure, a fierce need to match fire with fire and to respond to him with all the aching need that was building up within her. It would be hard to fight against herself and him—not that she wanted to.

Her mouth softened under his, and her heart accelerated wildly. Her hands found their way under his shirt as she touched him, rediscovering the hard contours of his body. His mouth left hers, burning hotly against her skin as he tilted her head back, devastating her senses as he slowly ravaged the supple column of her throat. He drew on the tender flesh and left his mark. His hand sought the supple feel of her breasts as he cupped them, rubbing his thumbs on her nipples. A strangled cry of pleasure escaped her lips as his lips followed his hands. The movement of his tongue was roughly erotic as it brushed the sensitive peaks of her breast. Her fingers bit protestingly into his shoulders.

Dandre' growled deep in his throat. The sensation of her hands on his flesh was so exquisite. Anjou's touch made Dandre' feel like he was going to explode from within. No one had ever affected him this way. It was as if he could not get enough of her. It seemed his hunger for her was unquenchable.

CHAPTER 5

Good Lord, the woman is fast becoming an addiction, he thought. Her hand smoothed the tousled hair on his head. Dandre' purred softly. He liked to be touched—or rather, he liked her touching him. He kissed her thoroughly, gently nipping at her lip before straightening up and gazing down at her beautiful face.

He whispered, "Mon cheri, honey, what would you like to do today?"

"I'd like you to take me home. I don't have any clothes to put on other than what I wore last night to the opera," Andy said.

"I like you naked. However, your wish is my command. You can take a shower, if you like." He walked towards the door. "I will take these dishes to the kitchen. See you in a few."

Andy stood in the shower as jets of water flowed over her naked body. Dandre' stood in the doorway and admired her beautiful curves, her long black hair flowing down her back, and her thighs with shapely legs. His manhood was already rock hard. In one swift movement, he removed his clothes, opened the door, and joined her in the shower. His heart was pounding so hard that he thought it would jump out of his chest. Dandre' had never taken a shower with a woman before; this was the first time. But then he realised there were a lot of firsts with Anjou.

The moment he stepped in the shower, he joined his mouth with hers, burying his long fingers into her hair as the water cascaded over their naked bodies. He closed his eyes and purred as he ravished her mouth with his. He engaged her tongue in a duel as he suckled and licked her. Dandre' then reached for the soap. As he began to lather their bodies, he ran his hand up her arms and across her chest. He drew circles around her breast. Her heart rate escalated with every stroke of his powerful hand.

"Turn and face the wall," Dandre' instructed her, a deep growling sound of hunger issued from his throat behind her. Andy closed her eyes. A hoarse, rumbling voice spoke from behind her and near her ear, sending delicious tremors down her spine. He wrapped her hair around his fingers, tugging her head back so their lips could touch. Andy moaned as his mouth descended and captured hers. He tasted of honey and spice. Dandre' released her hair and said, "Face the wall, mon cheri." His mouth skittered around her earlobe, his tongue swirling in its delicate fold. "And spread your legs." A muscular arm came around her waist to pull her back against him. The length of him was hard and hot, and he decisively thrust forward in one swift movement. He buried himself deep into her, and she felt him above her and behind her and in her as he established a rhythm. It seemed as if they were breathing together, warm water spraying down as he pumped hard and fast. His hand slid around her as he used his fingers to caress her feminine core.

Andy began to tremble as she felt the first wave of ecstasy hit her. She could take no more and began to scream. Her cries drove him on, unleashing the erotic and wild beast in him. He released a deep, throaty purr that triggered a response. She screamed his name and then sobbed when her body began to convulse. As the water poured down on them, she felt him release his seed in her womb. Hot, molten liquid flooded her. The sensation was so potent that it triggered another orgasm. Dandre' licked her earlobe as he whispered, "A moi pour toujours … Forever mine."

Andy slumped against the wall with Dandre' still buried deep inside her. Her desire for him was still hot and potent, and it flowed through her blood. *What is it about this man that makes me feel like I can't get enough of him?* she wondered.

Dandre' was still hard, and he began to move in her. Soon he established a rhythm as she moved with him. He reached up and began caressing her breast, and wild liquid fire began to race along her veins. She could feel his hot breath on her neck. Dandre' used his teeth to nip her as he suckled the sensitive area at the base of her neck, leaving his mark on her. He withdrew as he turned her around, lifting her up. "Wrap your legs around my waist, sweetheart," he instructed as he buried himself in her hot fold. Andy wrapped her legs around his waist as he walked over to the wall. Dandre' began to pump into her and stretched her. Andy's fingernails dug into his shoulders. The passion inside her was ignited. He thrust in and out, going deeper each time, driving her to the edge. Andy purred as she ran her fingers through his hair. Her action spurred him on, and he releases a deep, feral growled that triggered a response from her. Andy moaned as he took her deeper in the whirlpool of erotic pleasure.

Dandre' tossed his head back as a powerful orgasm tore through him, exploding inside her. He cupped her backside as he gave it all to her, calling out her name.

Andy kissed him, muttering, "My prince, oh, my prince,"

as she placed her head on his shoulder, too weak to do anything else. Dandre' gently lifted her out of the shower, wrapped her in a fluffy bath towel, and carried her to his bedroom, where they engaged in another heart-throbbing round of lovemaking. Andy fell asleep him his arms with a contented smile on her face.

Later on, in the afternoon, Dandre' took Andy home so she could change her clothes. Afterwards, he took her to a cookout at his grandparents' home. He pulled up in front of the Neilson residence a few minutes past noon. The weathered grey Victorian house sat on a few hundred acres of land with a well-manicured lawn. The driveway was graced with the most beautiful variety of roses.

The mahogany stained door had a beautiful wreath hanging on it. The moment Dandre' opened the door, Andy was assaulted with music, laughter, and the smell of food. She asked, "How I am supposed to act?"

"Just be your beautiful self," was his response.

"Well, what if they don't like me?"

"Relax. They will like you. Besides, what is there not to like about you? They are going to love you."

All the activities were at the rear of the house. Dandre' led her outside, looking for his grandmother. Later on, he took Andy by the hand as he gave her a tour of his grandparents' home. There were several photographs of his father and his siblings hanging near the fireplace. As Andy gazed at the photos, she could see the resemblances. Then there were photos of Dandre' and his siblings from kindergarten to university. Also, there were several group photos at different gatherings. Each photo captured the joy of the moment.

She was about to walk away when a silver frame caught her eyes. Andy reached out and picked it up. It was a younger version of Dandre' standing beside a small, twin-engine plane. "This was taken the day I got my pilot license," he explained.

"Oh. I had no idea you could fly."

He wrapped his arm around her waist. "There are a lot of things I can do, mon cheri," he said, chuckling.

Andy gave him a playful slap on the arm before responding, "I am sure there are."

She followed him into the family room. There were at least twenty people in the room sitting or standing, and everyone was talking. After taking her by the hand, he walked over to an older gentleman sitting on the settee. "Dad, I would like you to me someone very special to me. Anjou, this is my father, Dr Juan Neilson."

Andy extended her hand. "It's a pleasure to meet you, sir."

"Call me Juan," he said, giving her a big bear hug. "Dandre', your mother is in the kitchen with the rest of the ladies, cooking up a storm."

After that, Andy had difficulty keep up with all the names and faces; she hoped that there wouldn't be a test later. Andy was sitting on a bench under a June plum tree, enjoying the feel of the late-afternoon sun on her face. There was a sense of serenity as she watched the interactions of Dandre's family. Currently he was playing soccer with his cousins. She watched as he raced across the makeshift ninety-yard field to score a goal. He was a pure ball of endless energy, like the Energizer bunny. She wondered how he could be so energetic after all that lovemaking last night and this morning.

On their way home, Andy said, "It's easy to see why your grandparents have been married for over fifty years. I saw him swat your grandmother on her behind a few times."

"I bet he did," Dandre' said. "Colar walked in on them

kissing in the family room like two randy teenagers. Now I understand why they had nine children."

Giggling, Andy said, "Well, I should hope my husband would still be as frisky as your grandfather when he gets to be his age. You have a terrific family. Thank you for inviting me. I really like them and had a great time."

"You are welcome. They seem to like you too. I am glad you had a great time," he said, brushing his lips against hers.

"How was the opera?" Trista and Paige asked.

"It was fabulous," Andy replied. "I cried through the entire performance. It was beautiful and nostalgic, and Dandre' was the perfect gentleman: he held my hand the entire time. His touch was so soothing and reassuring."

"You're glowing," Gail said. "What's going on? There is something that you are not telling us. What did you guys do after the show?"

"OK, OK. I will tell you. After the show, we flew back, and I spent the night and entire day with him."

"You what?" Paige said.

"I spent the night with him," Andy repeated.

"Did you sleep with him?"

"Yes." Hot colour burned Andy's cheeks as she remembered their time together.

"It's about time," Gail said, giggling. "I was beginning to worry!"

"Why is that?" Andy asked.

"Because ever since things ended between you and Adam, you shut yourself off."

Before Andy could respond, Trista enquired, "Was it good? Can he bone?"

"Don't be so crass!" Paige said.

"Well, can he?" Marche asked.

"The man is a master at making love. He deserves a Golden Globe award. He wore me out! I am still trying to recover," Andy said with a smile.

"Ooh," chimed the others. "Tell us more."

"I don't want to talk about me," Andy said. "Let's talk about you. Ms Paige, from what I hear, a certain Mr Romeo is chasing after you."

"Who is that?" Gail asked.

Andy said, "Colar Neilson."

"You mean Dandre's sexy brother?"

"The one and only," replied Andy.

"I am not about to give Colar the time of the day," Paige replied. "I will admit the man is sexy as sin, but he is also a womaniser. I will not be his plaything or flavour of the month."

"I hear you," the others chimed.

"But still, you must be tempted just a little. Those eye and dimples are to die for," Trista said, giggling.

"So how is the design for Dandre's house and resort going?" Gail asked.

"It is great. As a matter of fact, I have completed the ones for his house. Now he is getting ready to take it to the builder." Do you believe he asked me to design twelve bedrooms?"

"Why so many?" Trista wanted to know.

"Well, according to Dandre', he wants to have five or six children."

"Spoken like a true Jamaican," Gail muttered.

"Speaking of which, are you guys ready for the fundraising gala the Board of Education is putting on?"

"Oh, yeah," Gail said. "I am really looking forward to it.

All the funds generated will go towards building the science lab at Monroe College. That's a worthy cause. Education is very important. I think twenty-five hundred dollars is a small price to pay for a ticket."

"Amen," chimed in Paige.

"So, when are you seeing the mighty Mr Neilson again?" Marconnets asked with a grin.

"Why do you call him that?" Andy asked.

"Well, for starters, he was able to seduce you to give him your virginity. Second, he wore you out. Third, you have this glow and look like a very satisfied woman. Shall I go on?"

"You are right about all of the above. Tonight, he is taking me to a wine tasting that his brother Colar is hosting."

After a few hours, Andy bade her friends goodbye, went home, and took a short nap before getting ready for the evening. When Dandre' arrived later that evening, Andy was ready and waiting. As she opened the door, as always her heart was beating so fast that it felt like the flutter of a bird's wings.

"Hello, lovely," Dandre' greeted.

"Hi," Andy replied.

"Are you ready to go?" he asked.

Andy nodded and reached for her purse, and she could not help noticing how fine he looked. He was wearing tobacco brown linen pants with a polo shirt a shade lighter, turning what should have been casual wear into a fashion statement. The expert cut of what he was wore intensified the colour of his eyes and emphasised his muscular arms and broad chest. *Oh, he smells so damned good …* Andy wanted to bury her face in his broad chest.

The drive to his brother's vineyard was very relaxing. Dandre's stereo released the sounds of Kenny G. As they approached the entrance, the sign read, "Chateau de Colar." The car came to a complete stop. Dandre' walked around the passenger door and released the seat belt. He assisted her as she exited the vehicle, and she was greeted with the fresh, exotic, heady smell of wine. Andy inhaled deeply. "This is so wonderful," she exclaimed.

Dandre' said, "I know what you mean."

As they walked towards the entrance, Colar emerged with a huge smile on his face. "Hello, Anjou. Welcome to Chateau de Colar." He gave her a huge hug and a kiss. "Come. I will give Andy a tour." For the next two hours, Andy listened to the deep baritone of Colar's voice as he explained the production and techniques of making and tasting different wines, and how it affected the palate.

Chateau de Colar was his unique brand of wine. He specialised in red, white, and rose. "Wine fermentation requires time," he stated. "Wine can ferment for three days or three years, depending on the style of wine you are trying to produce. Wine making or vinification, is the production of wine, starting with the selection of the grapes or other produce, and ending with bottling the finished wine. Although most wines are made from grapes, it may also be made from other fruits or plants.

"Wine making can be divided into two general categories: still wine production—that is, wine without carbonation—and sparkling wine production, with carbonation that can be natural or injected. The quality of grapes determines the quality of the wine more than any other factor. Grape quality is affected by variety, weather during the growing season, soil, minerals, acidity, time of harvest, and pruning method. The combination of these effects is often referred to as the grape's terroir.

"Containers are a major factor when fermenting the wine. Stainless steel and oak barrels are commonly used today. Each container imparts different factors in the wine's maturation. Grapes from the same vineyard will produce different wines when stored in different types of container. Red wines are made from black grapes and have a red or blue tint. Most grapes have a colourless juice, so to make red wine, the grape skins, which contain nearly all of the grape's pigmentation, have to remain intact with the juice during all or part of the fermentation process. Tannins are also found in the grape skins, and they are transferred into the wine while the skins are in contact with the juice.

"The primary difference between red and white wines is tannins, which are found mainly in red wines; they provide a dry, puckery sensation in the mouth and in the back of the throat. They also help preserve wine, allowing most but not all red wine to be aged longer than white wines. The red wines that we produce here are Beaujolais, Cabernet Sauvignon, Merlot, Pinot Noir, Zinfandel, and Chianti.

"On the other hand, rose wine is pink in colour and is also referred to as blush wine. Rose is made from black grapes, but it doesn't fully turn red because the grape skins are removed from the juice a few hours after contact. This brief contact with the grape skins gives the wine a pink colour from the slight transference of red pigments from the skins. Rose can also be made from blending together white and red wines. Many rose wines are sweet. White Merlot and White Zinfandel are a few great examples, however the most traditional European roses are very dry.

"How did you get started as a wine connoisseur?" Andy asked.

Colar chuckled. "As a child, my brothers and I spent our

summers in France with my granduncle, who has a vineyard. As the baby of the family, I used to follow him around. To say the least, I was spoilt rotten. He used to allow me to help with various chores. As I grew older, I realised that I loved wine. After finishing high school, I went to France and took my major in oenology. The rest, as they say, is history."

"I am really impressed. This is awesome," Andy said. "Now I know what it takes to produce wine. When I order a glass of wine with dinner, I will definitely have a new appreciation for it."

"At Chateau de Colar, there is also a wine club and barrel club, as well as a custom wine label service."

"Custom wine labels?" Andy repeated.

"Yes," Colar replied. "For visitors who seek an elegant, distinctive way to celebrate and mark a special event, we are able to create a custom label for them. For you, Anjou, we will stop by the wine market inside the winery and create a custom-labelled bottle of wine to celebrate your visit."

"Oh, that is awfully sweet of you," she said.

Colar laughed. "No problem. Dandre' will never forgive me if I didn't."

After the tour, Dandre' and Andy joined other guests to dine under the stars at the vineyard. Her taste buds transcended time with a celebration of local and international flavours presented by the chefs and winemakers. The evening kicked off with cocktails followed by a multi-course dinner paired with select wines.

Dandre' pulled into Andy's driveway. She turned to him and said, "I had a great time tonight. I don't know how to thank you."

"Well, I know of a way you can express your gratitude," he said with a grin.

"How?"

"You can start by kissing me," Dandre' said as he captured her mouth in a hot kiss.

Andy could not look at him without wanting him. Desire curled inside her abdomen as she remembered the things he had done to her during the night she had spent with him. She had no idea a man could have such devastating abilities. In no time he'd had her screaming in ecstasy and begging him for more. Andy had often thought she was independent, self-reliant, and reserved. She found it highly embarrassing that she could act like a wanton hussy. It was as if every fibre of her being had become sensitised all at once. It was as if Dandre' had transferred his own sexual energy to her, making himself vibrate throughout her body. The erotic surge was too much for her, causing her to have multiple orgasms. He was such a considerate lover, and the more he gave to her, the more lost she became. To be quite honest, he was worth the wait.

Afterwards, he had held her tenderly in his arms as he whispered in her ear wicked, naughty, erotic things in French. The soothing sexy timber of his voice had a spellbinding effect on her. Dandre' created a need in her that only he could satisfy, making her vulnerable. He was overpowering in his sensuality, personality, mastery, appearance, and command. She had never met anyone quite like him and wondered what she would do when their affair ended.

Slowly she pulled her mouth away. She was tingling all over. He had only to look at her with those sultry, smouldering golden eyes, and she was ready to surrender to his kisses and whatever he wanted to do to her. Andy thought, *This is not good.* She was confused about what was happening to her and was not sure what to make of the emotions she felt. She shook her head, said, "I have to go," and hastily exited the car. Dandre' watched as she inserted the key in the lock and open the door.

Andy closed the door behind her and leaned against it with her eyes closed, taking deep gulps of air as she tried to still her racing heart. Being around Dandre' caused her senses to come alive and be on fire. She was at a loss as to why he affected her this way. If she had stayed a moment longer in the car, she would have jumped his bones. "Oh boy. Talk about being whipped!" She stripped off her clothes as she headed for her bedroom. A cold shower would cool the liquid fire racing through her bloodstream.

It was Saturday. Andy and the girls were at Body by T, the all-inclusive health club at which they were members, playing tennis. "That was fantastic," Gail said. "That Sharon is a sore loser. I can't stand her uppity ass. That woman don't have a genuine bone in her body."

Just then, a voice from behind called out, "Who is Anjou?"

After turning around, all six women replied, "Who wants to know?"

Standing before them was a busty brunette.

"I am," Andy said, stepping forward. "Who are you?"

"Well, if you must know," the brunette replied while fluffing her hair, "I am Wendy, Dandre's fiancée."

"Really? Funny—he never mentions you," Andy replied.

"We had a little tiff before I left for Canada. He was sowing his wild oats and amusing himself with you while I was gone, which is OK. Now I am back, so do yourself a favour and get lost."

Stepping forward, Marche said, "Heifer, get stepping before you get a beatdown the likes of which you will never forget!"

Wendy took a couple of steps back before saying, "Dandre' is mine, and I will never let you have him." Then she sauntered away.

"Can you believe the nerve of that idiot?" Marconnets said.

Andy said, "Yeah, what is wrong with some of us women? I don't know. Now you see why I prefer to stay away from relationships! Some men can't be trusted. I don't need the drama and complication of being involved with any of them. I blame myself—Dandre' never made me any promises."

"Wait a minute," Trista said. "You don't know that this woman is telling the truth."

"For all we know, she may be an imposter. Dandre' is a very wealthy and eligible man, which means that vultures are attracted to him for more than one reason," Paige said.

"Precisely," Gail replied. "I think you should give him the benefit of the doubt.

"Please, Andy. Don't make any hasty decisions. Dandre' has a right to defend himself," Marche said. "Somehow I know she is lying. Now, let's go get something to eat. I am famished."

Dandre' hung the phone up in frustration. For several days, he had tried to reach Andy without success. Both her cell and home phones kept going to voicemail. To make matters worse, calling the office was no different; she was either in a meeting or unavailable, her assistant kept saying. Something was not right, and even more frustrating was that he was thousands of miles away from home.

While scratching his head in irritation, he dialled his brother Chayse's number.

"Hello?"

"Chayse, it's me, Dandre'."

"Hey. What's going on?"

"I am frustrated as hell, man! I have tried to reach Anjou for several days. Now I think she is avoiding my calls. Do you know what's going on?"

Chayse chuckled. "It's not what but who."

"What do you mean?"

"Wendy is back, and she had the audacity to confront Andy at the health club, warning her to stay away from you."

"Really? It's been over for three years between me and her. I wonder what kind of sick game she is playing this time."

"I would not worry about it," Chayse said. "Women like Wendy have problems. They don't know what real love or relationships are about. They are as shallow as the bay at Eagle's Point. Then they have the nerve to complain about not finding a good man."

"Oh, I am not worried at all," Dandre' said in a deadly voice. "I will take care of Miss Wendy. Where does she get off thinking she has a right to lay claim on me? I swear, Chayse, Wendy will regret the day she approached Anjou. That is why she is not taking my calls?"

"Yeah, Dandre'. But Andy has no way of knowing that there is nothing going on between you and Wendy. Considering what she had gone through with her ex-boyfriend, I understand why she may feel like history is repeating itself. Does Andy know how you feel about her?"

"No," Dandre' admitted.

"What in the hell is wrong with you? What good are your feelings if she doesn't know about them? No wonder she is not taking your calls."

Dandre' sighed. "I guess you are right. I will straighten this mess out when I get home."

"Yes, be sure that you do. I would hate for things to get messed up between you and Anju just because some silly female can't let go. I am rooting for you, man. All of us are. When you coming home?" Chayse asked.

"Now. I was going to leave on Friday, but given the situation, Jonas can finish up the negotiations. My woman needs me, and I am coming to take care of her. I know that's right."

"OK, see you later."

"Thanks, man. Bye."

CHAPTER 6

The door to Andy's office was open. Dandre' leaned against the door frame, his ankles cross and both hands in his pockets. He watched her as she bent over the diagram on her desk. She was not aware that he was there. Suddenly, an image flashed through his mind with him taking her in that position.

He must have made a sound because Andy's body became tense the moment she became aware of his presence. She stood up straight and said, "Go away, Dandre'. You are not welcome here."

"Hello, mon cheri. It's good to see you too," he said while strolling towards her.

"Don't you dare call me that!" she hissed through clenched teeth.

His heart swelled with love as he gazed at her. *She is just as beautiful angry as she is calm,* he thought. "We need to talk." He was dressed in a charcoal suit with a light blue shirt. The first few buttons on his shirt were open, revealing the powerful column of his neck.

Andy's heart was beating so fast that she could hear it. The intensity in his eyes made heat pool between her legs as shivers danced up and down her spine. She crossed her arms over her chest and said, "Why you don't go back to your fiancée before she gets worried?"

"I don't have a fiancée."

"You don't? Could have fooled me," replied Andy as she went back to studying the diagram on her desk.

Dandre' reached out and pulled Andy to him. "Listen, mon amour. Wendy and I broke up over three years ago, and I have not seen her since. I am sorry you had to deal with her, but believe me, Anjou, I have no interest or desire for another woman."

She lifted an arched brow. "Why?"

Dandre' sighed. He could see she was going to be difficult.

"Look, Dandre'. It's OK. You don't have to let me down gently. I understand you never made me any promises. I was the fool, thinking we had something special. I know it was fun while it lasted." Andy turned her head so Dandre' would not see the pain in her eyes. "You are free to go."

"For God's sake, woman. Will you be quiet and listen to me for a minute?" Andy stopped talking and turned her head to look at Dandre'. "So you think I am here to end our relationship?"

"Aren't you?" she asked. The softness of her voice tugged at Dandre's heart, and he regretted more than ever that he'd never expressed to her how much she meant to him.

After taking a deep breath, Dandre' pulled Andy into his arms. "I am so sorry. I should have told you how I felt the night we went to New York, but I am going to tell you now. Anjou, from the moment I saw you at Sunset Negril, I knew you were the one. I love you. For me, there is no other. All I ask of you is that you wake up in the morning, and I will take it from there. If the world was mine to give, I would give it to you. All that your heart desires, I will spend the rest of my days making sure you have it. I love you, Anjou.

Will you marry me and be my baby mama? Will you grow old with me?"

Andy was speechless. Dandre' was on his knees, and in his hand was the largest diamond ring she had ever seen. Andy knelt down too and threw her arms around Dandre's neck. "Yes, I will marry you! I will be your baby mama, and it would be my honour to grow old with you." She took hold of his stunning face and forced him to look at her. Andy kissed him fast, taking him by surprise.

His lids lowered as his gaze fixed on her lips. There was a new depth to the exchange. Dandre' held her close, and a wild passion built inside him. They were both becoming hot and bothered, and they both moaned. Dandre' stood pulling Andy to her feet. "I'd better leave before I lose control. You are still at the office."

Andy smiled and walked towards her desk. "That can be remedied." She picked up her phone. "Mrs Gray, please hold all calls."

"Yes, Ms Royale."

Andy walked towards Dandre', taking off her jacket and placing it on the back of her chair. "Well, Mr Neilson, would you like to play?"

In one swift move, Dandre' picked up Andy and carried her to the couch that was at the far end of her office. He gently laid her on the couch and unbuttoned her blouse. With one flick of his wrist, he unclasped the hook on her bra. White teeth captured the jutting tip of her breast, and he suckled vigorously. Her eyes fluttered shut, and a sound of raw desire ripped from her. The intense sound reverberated through Dandre', and in a graceful move he pushed her skirt above her thighs and up to her waist. After removing his suit and undergarment, Dandre's hand cupped the back of her thigh as he lifted her, bringing her flush against his desire. He thrust in her with long, penetrating strokes and began to massage her inside.

She was still very tight due to the newness of the experience. Her muscles clamped him tightly with fluid agility. He changed her angle by bringing her legs from around his hips, positioning them straight under him. Their breathing accelerated wildly. Dandre' thrust in and out. Andy began to move to the beat of the rhythm that he established. As a wave of ecstasy built, he began to pulse in her. The sensation vibrated through her entire being. Andy screamed, and Dandre' captured her lips as he absorbed her moan. He rotated his hips, pressing more fully as he flexed inside her. The sensation was too much, and Andy began to purr deep in her throat. His long hair swung forward as he murmured throatily into her mouth, "Mon cheri, do you like it?" Withdrawing halfway, he captured her lip with a sexy little tug and then slid in her as far as he could go.

"Dandre'!" she gasped. He pulled her hips up sharply as he bore down just a little, touching her G spot. "Oh my." Andy came apart, scraping her nails down his back. A low growl resonated from his throat. While holding her still, he gave her another peak by rotating hard against her dampness. "Yes, please!" Andy begged as a gigantic orgasm ripped through her. The sensation was so intense. Dandre' throw his head back as he reached his peak of fast and powerful release, all the muscles straining in his neck as he slumped on top of her.

After rising on his arm, Dandre' gave her face a long and sensuous lick before standing up, sitting up dazedly. Andy placed her hand over her heart and said, "That was amazing … I thought I had died and gone to heaven."

Dandre' winked at her as he gave a wicked grin. "You

should get some work done." He had made love to her again with just a bathroom break in between. There was no doubt in Andy's mind that he could keep going. The man had a stamina that was second to none, and she wondered if all men were like him.

She was worn out; truthfully, she needed a nap. Andy stared at his sensuous lips, remembering their velvety touch and the exquisite pleasure they gave. "You are right. You should go. I do have a lot of work to do."

Dandre' kissed her hard on the mouth. "Dinner tonight. I will pick you up at 7:30," he said as he walked out the door.

Andy lifted her left hand to look at the engagement ring on her finger. *How did he know I love blue diamonds?* she wondered. Andy picked up her phone and dial Marche's number.

"Hello?"

"Marche, this is Andy. Will you call all the girls and meet me at Cousins for lunch at one o'clock?"

"Sure. What's going on?

"You will see."

"OK, see you then."

Two hours later Andy, her sisters, and her friends were led to their table at the restaurant. While glancing around, Andy noticed that the patrons were mostly dress in business suits. The restaurant was a popular place, and many business luncheons took place there. They were sitting towards the back of the restaurant, and the atmosphere was relaxing as soft jazz flowed through the surround system.

"Well, sis, we are all here. What's going on?" Marconnets asked.

Andy could hear the anxiety in her sister's voice. "Nothing

is wrong," Andy quickly reassured them. "I just wanted to share some news with you guys. I saw Dandre' earlier today."

"He is back from France?" Trista asked.

"Yes."

"Well, what did you do, Andy?" Marche asked. "Please tell me you did not break up with him."

"I tried, but it did not work. You were right: there was nothing going on between him and Wendy. He said they broke up three years ago, and he has not seen her since."

"Told you," Gail said. "I knew she was lying."

"That heifer. I still say you should have let me give her a beatdown," Marche said, giggling.

Andy rolled her eyes. "We know Wendy would be no match for you. The reason why I asked you guys here is so that we might celebrate."

"Celebrate?" Paige asked.

"Yes," Andy replied, lifting her left hand for all to see. "Dandre' proposed, and I accepted!"

"Proposed!" the women said in unison.

"Oh my God. This rock is huge!" Trista squeaked.

Gail signalled their waitress and ordered a bottle of Dom Pérignon.

"So have you guys set a wedding date yet?" Paige asked.

"No," Andy replied. "We just got engaged. I wanted you guys to know. Mommy and Daddy already knew—Dandre' asked for their blessing before he came to see me."

"He is such a gentleman!" Marconnets said. "We really do need more men like him."

"Yeah, I believe from the first day Mom met Dandre', he stole her heart. I am excited about this wedding," Marconnets said. "There will be so much to do. Just think about going shopping for the wedding dress and planning the entire thing."

Andy chuckled. "I am not a fan of big weddings."

"You may not be, but your parents are. Besides, both you and Dandre' are from large families," Trista said.

"Speaking of which I am, going shopping on Saturday for the fundraising ball. I was wondering if you guys would like to join me."

"I definitely will," Gail said. "I need a dress."

"Amen," Marche said.

The girls chatted for a while and enjoyed their lunch before going back to their respective jobs.

Later that evening, Andy called and spoke with her parents. As always her father asked, "How are you doing, sweet pea?"

"I am fine, Daddy," she replied.

"Your young man came by yesterday to ask for your hand. I really like Dandre'. I believe he will make you very happy."

"Thanks, Daddy. I am glad to know that you and Mommy like him."

Her father chuckled. "Your mother adores him. To her he is another son. I and your brothers are going white-water rafting, and we have invited Dandre'."

"I am sure that is something that he would enjoy," Andy said. She conversed with her father for a while before ending the call.

Dandre' was vaguely aware of the information that Jonas was giving him about his recent acquisition of the aviation company. Jonas was one of his marketing managers Dandre' had left him in France to close the deal.

"So as you can see, Mr Neilson, everything is as you

expected. The documents have been signed, and our attorneys will be contacting you later today."

"Thank you, Jonas. I appreciate you and the work that you have done. I knew I could count on you."

A huge grin broke out on Jonas's face. "I enjoy working for Triple X Aviation. How often do you get to do what you love and work for a great company?"

"Speaking of which I need a CEO for the French branch. Would you be interested in the position?" Dandre' asked. "You don't have to give me an answer now. If you need a few days to think about it, that is fine. Just let me know by Monday afternoon."

"I definitely will let you know," Jonas said with a smile as he headed for the door.

A few hours later, Dandre's phone rang. "Mr Neilson, your brothers are here to see you."

"Thank you, Jackie. You can send them in."

"Howdy, Dandre'."

"Hi, guys. What's up?" Dandre' said.

"Just checking up on you," Christopher replied.

"I hear congratulations are in order," Colar said with a cheeky grin.

"Thanks," Dandre' replied.

"Damn, I can't believe that in less than a year, I am losing two of my brothers to marriage," Colar mourned.

"Maybe you should try it," Chayse said.

"Hell, no. I am not getting married anytime soon. There are too many fine honeys for me to settle with one. I like them all. Giving up my player card is not an option at this time."

"I swear, Colar. Sometimes I wonder whether a pack of

wolves dropped you at Mom and Dad's doorstep," Christopher said, rolling his eyes.

"Don't mind him," Dandre' said. "I know there is a certain redhead named Paige that he has the hots for … and from what I hear, she is not giving his sorry ass the time of the day!"

"Did you ever hear the saying, 'The man who laughs last laughs best'? Patience, brother dear. Paige is mine—you will see," Colar said.

Dandre' said, "Paige is Anjou's friend, and if you hurt her, you will have to answer to me. The way I see it, if your intentions towards Paige are no good, I suggest you leave her alone."

"Whatever, man," Colar said, laughing.

"So when is the big day?" Chayse asked.

"We have not set a date yet, but I am sure it will be after the house is finished." I am happy for you," Christopher said. "Marriage is one of the best things that has ever happened to me, and if you can experience half the happiness that Melody brings me, then I say go for it."

"Thanks. I appreciate it," Dandre' said. "Andy did an excellent job in designing the house."

"It was ingenious of you to have her create the plan."

Dandre' grinned. "Yeah, it was only right that she did. After all, she is going to be the queen of the castle. I knew I was going to marry her, but at the time I could not say that to her. She would have run for cover! Hell, I could not even get her to go on date with me." He chuckled. "Chris, you remember when you met Melody, and how it took a while to get her to go out with you?"

"Yeah. She lived and breathed her work and had no

interest in dating, much less getting married. What is it with us men, falling for difficult women?" Christopher mused.

"Anything that is so unique, beautiful, and special is worth fighting for," Dandre' said. "If it took me a million years to win her heart, I would keep at it."

"OK, guys," Chayse said. "Enough. I am hungry. Can we go grab a bite?"

"That sounds good to me," Colar said.

"Well, I am glad that you are getting ready to tie the knot," Chayse said as they exited Dandre's office.

Yeah," Colar said. "It takes the focus off us for a while. No more talk from Mommy about her wanting grandchildren. Right now, she is happy to be planning another wedding."

"Little brother, I think you should try to behave yourself."

Colar laughed. "What can I say? It's not my fault that the honeys adore me."

"Boy, you are conceited," Christopher grumbled. "You think you are the best thing since sliced bread."

Dandre' burst out laughing. "He sure has a chip on his shoulder, doesn't he? I'll tell you one thing: Romeo is going to fall, and when he does, he is going to fall hard."

"Now, that I will have to see," Christopher said.

"I think he is halfway way there," Chayse noted.

"Mind your damn business," Colar said. "I hate it when you talk about me as if I am not here. And for your information, I am not in love with Paige."

The three brothers crossed their arms and looked at their youngest brother. "What do you mean, you are not in love with Paige?" Christopher asked.

"I told you once before," Dandre' said. "If your intentions are not good towards her, then leave alone."

"If we had a sister, would you want a man to have a fling

with her, breaking her heart and then discarding her like an old shoe when something else comes along?" Chayse asked. "Think before you answer, because if you say anything other than what is right, I will beat the hell out of you."

"I never lead a woman on," Colar said. "I have always been honest with them about where things stand before we get involve."

"Really? And you want us to believe that? You have never had a serious relationship, so how is this any different? Paige is practically family. She is Anjou's best friend. Do you know the impact that would have on Anjou if you hurt Paige?"

"Who says I am going to hurt Paige? I really care about her, but I am not in love with her."

"Then the answer is no, you can't date her," Christopher said, chuckling.

Colar replied, "I don't need your permission. I can date whomever I damn well please."

"That is where you are wrong, little brother. You can't say you have not been warned. Stay away from Paige until you can admit that you love her. Until then, you must leave her be."

Colar said, "Who died and made you her keeper? The last time I checked, she is a grown woman who can make her own decisions. Whatever transpires between me and Paige is none of your business. Now, are we going to lunch?"

CHAPTER 7

Andy was so excited. Today, she and Dandre' were schedule to visit Duranta Repens Estate, the place where their dream home was being built. Andy was excited for more than one reason. The major one was she'd designed the house. When Dandre' had approached her with the proposal to design his home, she'd had no idea he would ask her to marry him. There was a certain satisfaction and pride that she experienced every time one of her creations on paper became a reality. This house was nestled on seventy-five acres of land with an oceanfront view and a private beach. She designed the single-style mansion with a European design, a cathedral ceiling, a master suite with en suite bath, and an office on the main floor. Six bedrooms, each with private baths, were situated upstairs. There was a teen suite with kitchen, living room, bedroom, and bath above a three-car garage. She designed a chef's kitchen with butler pantry to the banquet size dining room. There was also a breakfast room and a keeping room off the kitchen. The floors were done in beautiful marble tile with a double winding staircase, along with a french window and doors that opened to a lavish courtyard.

On the lower level, there were four other bedrooms, two and a half baths, a game room with a bar, and a theatre that seated about twenty people; Dandre' insisted on a mini gym with an indoor tennis court. Although the nights in Negril during the summer could be cool, the days were known to be hot, and so central air was installed. The appliances were all modern and state-of-the-art. Andy knew the history of the estate and how it had gotten its name, and so she had a beautiful garden designed to capture the lush, exotic, tropical flowers, chief of which were Duranta Repens.

Andy leaned back in her seat and closed her eyes, thinking how much her life had changed in eight months. She was sitting beside the most gorgeous man that had ever graced the planet, and she could truthfully say he belonged to her. She had a family that loved her and a very successful business. *Life is good. What more can a girl ask for?* She glanced over at Dandre' as he effortlessly manoeuvred the car towards their destination. In some faraway recess of her mind, Andy felt like all this was a beautiful dream. Sometimes she pinched herself to make sure she was awake.

Moments later, Dandre' pulled up to the gate, and the security guard smiled at them as they drove through. Dandre' brought the car to a stop halfway up the driveway. "Come on," he said. "I would like to walk the rest of the way to the house." As he assisted Andy out of the car, he took her hand in his and brought it to his lips in a tender kiss. Heat immediately flowed through her as his lips touch her fingers. "Do you have any idea how much I love you?" he said as they walked towards their home.

"No," Andy said with a giggle.

"No?" Dandre' repeated in disbelief. "Well, I guess I will just have to show you!" He gave a sly grin.

"Yeah, you do that," she countered. "I can't wait."

As Dandre' and Andy strolled through different areas

of the house, he asked, "Are you going to use a professional decorator, or do you plan on doing it yourself?"

She replied, "I know just the person to ask. I think he will have a field day at it."

"He?" Dandre' said.

"Yes. My brother Nicholas went to school with his sister. You may have heard of him. The company is called "Interiors by Beau.""

"Oh yes. I have heard of him, and I have seen his work. He is extremely talented," Dandre' said.

"So does that mean you approve?"

"My heart, whatever you decide is fine with me. I trust your judgement." He pulled her into his arms.

"In that case, you know what I have decided? I think we should christen every room in this house, starting with the master suite."

Dandre' raised an eyebrow. "That can be arranged, my little temptress." He pulled her down on the plush white carpet. Dandre' gave her mouth a sensuous lick before he captured her lip between his teeth.

Andy gasped as he slid his tongue in her mouth, and she purred deep in her throat. Her breasts throbbed, her nipples tingled, and her skin hummed with arousal. The curls between her legs were drenched. She wanted him so much that she ached. "Please, my prince, make love to me," she breathed.

Dandre' entangled his fingers in her hair to capture her mouth in a molten-hot kiss. As he slid fast in her hot depth, Andy threw her head back and cried out at the sensual torture. Every thrust, every stroke brought her such exquisite pleasure. Andy felt like she was drowning in a sea of ecstasy.

Dandre' captured one of her nipples in his huge hand as

he rubbed his thumb over the sensitive tip. "Is it too much?" he asked her.

"No," she gasped.

He winked lazily at her. "How about this?" he said as he pulsed in her.

Andy screamed as a gigantic orgasm ripped through her. "Oh my! Please!" she purred as she dug her nails in his back, which triggered an exquisite sensation in him. A low growl escaped his lips. While holding her immobile, he ground his hips by rotating hard against her wetness, triggering another orgasm. The sensation was too much for her, and Andy screamed. Dandre' threw his head back as he reached his own satisfaction, calling out her name.

Sometime later, lying at home in her bed, Andy was going over in her mind the different colour schemes for various parts of the mansion, and possible which Disney characters she would use to decorate the nursery. She figured if Dandre' continued at the rate he was going, it wouldn't be long before his friskiness produced an unplanned pregnancy. The thought did not bother her one bit because she knew any child born to her and Dandre' would be the product of their love. *The man is so gifted in the art of making love that it should be patented.* Chuckling at the idea, Andy rolled onto her stomach, closed her eyes, and went to sleep.

It was 5.00 a.m. in the morning when Dandre' got in his truck to head over to Andy's parents' home. Today he was going white-water rafting with her father and three brothers. He was excited, to say the least. Before he could knock on the door, Anita, Andy's mom, opened the door with a smile on her face. "Good morning, Dandre'." She stepped back to allow him to enter and closed the door behind her. He could smell the fresh Johnny cake. Ackee and salt fish assaulted his nostrils as he stepped in the kitchen, and his mouth watered.

"I hope you have not eaten. I have prepared breakfast for all of you," Anita said, turning to face him. For the millionth time, Dandre' was captivated by his future mother-in-law's beauty: her high cheekbones, waist-length black hair with a touch of silver at her temple, and hazel eyes. Andy, Marconnets, and Marche was the splitting image of their mother. The Indian, Egyptian, and African blood was very dominant. She was high yellow in complexion, also known as Mulatto. The woman was breathtaking. Her voice has a soothing melody to it.

Dandre' realised he had not answer her question. He cleared his throat and said, "No, Mom, I have not had breakfast yet."

"Good. Come," she said, leading the way to the breakfast room "Colee'rt and the boys are waiting for you."

"Good morning," Dandre' said as he entered the room.

"Good morning, son," Andy's father said.

"Good morning," Nicholas, Andre, and Noel said in unison.

"Ready to go rafting?" Andre asked.

"Yes," Dandre' replied. "I was so excited that I could hardly sleep last night."

Colee'rt chuckled. "I know what you mean. I was excited too and could hardly wait. There is something about going white-water rafting on a bamboo raft on the Martha Brae River. The feeling is second to none."

"Hey, Dad, tell Dandre' what we have lined up for the entire day and night."

"I hope you brought a change of clothes, because we are camping out tonight. There will be a party on the beach in

Mo Bay, and after the party we are usually too wasted to drive back. Drinking all of Ms Martha's homemade rum punch gets you in a very mellow state, if you know what I mean," Colee'rt said with a chuckle.

After breakfast, the men headed out to the yard to load their belongings in Colee'rt's truck. Anita walked outside to see them off. Dandre' and the boys watched as she wrapped her arms around her husband's neck, and the two shared a passionate kiss. As Anita stepped back from her husband, he playfully swatted her on the behind and muttered, "I love you, Nita."

She replied, "And I love you too, Collee."

The Martha Brae River was located three miles from the town of Falmouth and twenty miles from Montego Bay. Colee'rt had a thirty-foot raft made from pure bamboo that was already waiting for them at the pier. They boarded under the supervision of a licensed dispatcher. The raft ride was operated over an eight-mile stretch of the beautiful Martha Brae River and lasted for two to three hours. It offered a fully appointed recreational facility, which included picnic grounds, a full-service bar, three souvenir shops, a swimming pool, and modern restrooms. They planned to visit Ms Martha's Herb Garden, a preservation of Jamaica's herbs famous for their medicinal purposes.

As always, Dandre' was swallowed up by Jamaica's natural beauty. Bamboo rafts were originally used to transport produce, especially bananas, from the interior of the island. It was said that the legendary Hollywood star Errol Flynn, who made Port Antonio his home, introduced rafting for fun. Today, Martha Brae and Rio Grande rafting was an established attraction enjoyed by tourists and Jamaicans alike.

After Dandre' and his companions got back to the pier, they went to one of the bungalows that were on the beach for lunch. The rich aroma of grilled lobster; jerk chicken; roast fish stuffed with Callaloo green peppers, thyme, and other herbs; roasted yellow yams; and bammy assailed their senses. It reminded the men that they had not eaten since 6.00 a.m. Colee'rt led to the back of the restaurant, where he was greeted by the owner, his good friend Jimmy. The men greeted each other with bear hugs and slaps on the back.

"How you doing, Colee'rt? Long time, no see," Jim said.

"I am doing fine, Jim. How is the missus doing today?"

"She is good. Let me show you to your table, and I will have some Red Stripe beer brought to you."

Andre leaned over to Dandre' and said, "Uncle Jimmy and Daddy went to school together. The two are best friends and were as thick as thieves back in the day. I hear they were the confirmed players in Montego Bay until Mom captured Dad's heart. A year later, Uncle Jimmy met Auntie Merle, and the next thing you know, he was marching down the aisle. Uncle Jimmy used to brag that there was no woman who could capture his heart and make him give up his womaniser card. Today, he is still head over heels in love with her. They have four children, which you will meet at your wedding. Uncle Jimmy owns this restaurant, and he has several all over the north coast."

As Dandre' watched the interaction, he could tell there was a deep bond that went beyond mere friendship between his father-in-law and Uncle Jimmy. Dandre' glanced around the crowded restaurant. The ambiance was lively as patrons interacted with each other. Lunch was amazing, and Dandre' enjoyed the way Nicholas, Andre, and Noel related to each other. He could tell that the brothers were close and respected their father immensely. While looking at all four men, he could see that they were related; it reminded him of the relationship he shared with his brothers.

After lunch, the men left the restaurant and strolled along the beach. Dandre' stopped under a mango tree and glanced around the crowded beach. He thought nothing was more beautiful than Jamaica's North Coast. The fresh smell of the Caribbean Sea mingled with the rich aroma of exotic fruits, and food was something he would never get tired of. Suddenly he wished Anjou was with him. He reached in his pocket for his cell phone and used voice command to dial her number. As he waited for her to answer, he wondered what she was doing.

On the third ring, she answered. "Hello?"

"My heart," Dandre' said, "how are you?"

"Hi, honey." A smile touched Andy's lips as she heard Dandre's voice. I am fine."

"What are you doing?" he asked

"I was just getting ready to head over to Mom's. We are having a sleepover tonight with Melody, Gail, Paige, and Trista. Are you having fun with Daddy and my brothers?"

"Yes," Dandre' said, "but I miss you like crazy. I just wanted to hear your voice."

"I miss you too," she said. She could hear the longing in his voice, which triggered something inside her. "I will see you tomorrow."

"I love you," Dandre' said. "Dream of me tonight."

"I love you too. Bye."

As Dandre' hung up the phone, he knew he would be dreaming of Andy tonight. He placed his cell phone in his pocket and headed towards the others.

"Is everything OK, son?" Colee'rt asked.

"Yes, sir," Dandre' replied. "All is well. I was talking to Anjou. I missed her and just wanted to hear her voice."

The older man chuckled and said, "I know the feeling. Despite being married to her mother for nearly forty years, the woman still makes me weak at the knees. I am hopelessly in love with my Anita and can't imagine my life without her."

"How did you to meet?" Dandre' asked.

"At a youth rally. She was doing her third year at Shortwood Teachers College, and I was completing my master's in business at the College of Arts, Science, and Technology. She was with a group of interns, each carrying a sign that read 'One way Jesus'."

As Dandre' looked at Colee'rt, he could see that the man went back in time. There was this look on his face. Even though Dandre' could not explain it, he knew it because it was the same look he had on his face when he saw Anjou for the first time.

"I remember she was so passionate about Jesus. There was a fire that burned in her eyes as a devout Roman Catholic. I knew nothing about Jesus and salvation, but that night as she gave her testimony about the love of God and how He came to save us, I knew that not only did I need the Jesus she was talking about, but I needed her too. I fell in love instantly and completely with her. After the service was over, a group went to Road Runner to buy ice cream. I had no knowledge of this. I walked in thinking I had to see her again. Somehow to my surprise, there she was with the youth pastor, eating rocky road ice cream. I walked over to where they were sitting and introduced myself. They invited me to join them. For more than four hours, they sat and talked about Jesus, college life, and what they would do after graduation. Because the two colleges were nearby, the youth fellowship met every Friday night.

"We were inseparable after graduation. I had to return here, and she was still in Kingston, finishing. Every weekend I would drive to Kingston to see her. Prior to meeting Anita, I had roving eyes and was elusive and wild at heart. Now I only have eyes for her. I believe that there is one woman who can capture the heart of any man. It does not matter how wild he is when he meets her; he will know this is it. He has met his destiny, and he will turn in his player's card."

Dandre' looked at his future father-in-law and nodded, understanding exactly what the older man was saying. He truly met his destiny when he saw Anjou that night at Sunset Negril.

The night air was balmy. There was a cool breeze blowing over the island as Dandre' watched the night festivities. The Reggae music was blasting from the speakers of Stone Love, one of the island's own local entertainers from Kingston. A petite blonde walked up and asked Dandre' for a dance. He glanced at the others before accepting her hand. Soon all the others were dancing because the blonde, whose name was Patti, had a group of women with her who got a little boldness to approach the others. They were tourists visiting from Europe. Patti informed him that they were filming a movie, and their producers would use this beach party for one of the live scenes in the movie.

Later on, as Dandre' was standing and talking to Noel, Wendy strolled over with her shoes in her hand. She stopped in from of Dandre' and said, "I see you are not with your little girlfriend. I told her it was just a matter of time before you would become bored with her. You knew I would be here."

She purred as she touched his face and rubbed her breast on his chest.

"What the hell?" Noel roared.

"It's OK, Noel," Dandre' said. "Let me handle this crazy-ass woman." He captured Wendy's wrist in his large hand. "Keep your paws to yourself, Wendy, and don't flatter yourself. For your information, Anjou is not my little girlfriend, as you put it. She is my fiancée, the woman I love, and the woman I intend to marry. Don't ever make the mistake and talk to her again with your craziness. If you do, I promise you will live to regret it. We broke up over three years ago. Anjou is more woman than you will ever hope to be. What's the matter? Your boy-toy lover is unable to satisfy you?" He released her wrist. "Now, if you don't mind, I would like to get back to the conversation I was having with my brother-in-law before I was rudely interrupted. Run along before you make a bigger fool of yourself."

Noel burst out laughing. "Remind me never to cross you, my friend. I could not have handled that any better."

Wendy hurriedly walked away as she realised a small crowd had gathered around them.

"Have some more rum punch," Nicholas said as he handed Dandre' and Noel a glass each. The rest of the night passed without incident as the men danced, laughed, chatted, and had some good old-fashioned fun. When they left the beach, it was 4.30 a.m. as they headed for their tent.

CHAPTER 8

Colar exhaled a frustrating breath. Tonight was the fundraising ball at the Half Moon Hotel's grand ballroom. All proceeds would go towards the building of the science lab at Monroe College. What irritated him more than anything was that he had been trying to get Paige to go out with him for months but each invitation was met with a "double no". What the hell was that? A simple "No, thank you" would suffice.

A few days ago he had tried to get her to attend the ball as his date. Instead, she'd informed him that she would meet him there. He had not pushed for more because to his way of thinking, that was a small victory. Colar had no intention of leaving the ball without Paige at his side.

Paige glanced around the huge ballroom filled with people of all walks of life. Andy was right: VIPs from all over the island were attending the fundraising gala to give their financial support for Monroe College. It was rumoured that the persons or organization that donated the most would have their names engraved in what was known as the hall of fame at the college. She chuckled as she thought about some of Negril's wealthiest socialites competing to outgive each other.

Tonight she had caught a ride with Trista because she had promised Colar that she would meet him at the ball. She wondered for the millionth times whether she was doing the right thing. Ever since the night she'd seen Colar at Sunset Negril, he had been in relentless pursuit of her. It was not that she did not like him. It was simply that he had a reputation of being a womaniser. To make matters worse, he made her weak at the knees, and the sexual chemistry between them was off the charts. As she gazed around the room, she saw Colar and his brothers standing together with Tyler, Dandre's best friend, and Jonas, the AVP of Triple X Aviation. Andy; her sisters; her brothers Nicholas, Andre, and Noel; her parents; and Colar's parents looking at the older man. One could tell that he was related to Colar, Gail, and Melody. Christopher's wife was also there.

As Paige and Trista made their way towards them, she could feel the sizzling heat radiating from Colar's gaze. It was as if they were the only two people in the universe. She was wearing a two-piece sleeveless Sapphire blue taffeta gown with a heavily beaded bodice and a mermaid skirt, which emphasised her hips and long legs. The gown was stunning and showed off every one of her curves to perfection. Dangling from her ears were teardrop diamond earrings. Her hair was styled in a sophisticated updo that emphasised the slenderness of her neck.

"You are the most stunning creature. When Colar sees you tonight, he is going to have a heart attack," Trista told her. "Not to mention that every man in the room will want to steal you from him."

"I can't wait to see his face." Paige thought Trista was the one who was stunning. Andy, her sisters, and Gail were gorgeous in their gowns and jewellery.

Colar's breath caught in his throat. He realised that no other woman had ever made him experience this—the erotic beating of his blood rushing in his ears. *Damn, Paige is breathtaking.* From the corner of his eye, he could see Chayse grinning from ear to ear. He knew that his brother would not let him live this down in the days to come.

To prove him right, Chayse leaned over and whispered, "It looks like you have been knocked off your feet by a woman." He had a smug look on his face.

Colar glared at him. Chayse chuckled and grabbed a glass of champagne from a passing waiter.

Paige was not oblivious to Colar's reaction to her, and she smile inwardly. Her little shopping trip with Andy and the girls had paid off. All six women had an amazing lunch before heading for the salon, where they had manicures, pedicures, facials, and massages. After that, Trista insisted that they go shopping, and they entered this exclusive boutique that carried only designer outfits. That was when she saw her gown and knew that this was the one for her. She felt amazing when she tried it on, and by the time it was all over, the women had found beautiful gowns to wear. Trista suggested that she spend the night at her place so they could get ready together, and because Paige was riding with her, she agreed.

"I know it may be a little over the top, but we have a make-up artist and hair stylist coming tomorrow. I want to be drop-dead gorgeous when I walk into the ballroom tomorrow night," Trista said with a giggle.

Paige walked towards the others and stopped directly in front of Colar. "Hello," she said in a breathless whisper.

"Hi, Paige. You look amazing."

"Thank you. You don't look so bad yourself," she replied. She was about to walk away when she felt someone tug on her arm.

"Is that you, Paige?" a woman's voice said from behind.

"Yes," she answered.

"It's Beverley. We went to school together, remember?"

Paige knew exactly who she was. They had been friends for years, but Beverley had to move to Kingston when her father was transferred, and they had lost contact." It's so good to see you, Beverley. It's been a long time." Paige hugged her childhood friend. "You look amazing."

Beverley giggled. "And you are fabulous. Who is this handsome man?"

Paige released her hold and turned to introduce Colar. They chatted for a while, exchanged numbers, and promised to keep in touch with each other. "I am off to find some drop-dead, mouth-watering man to whisk me to paradise," Beverley told her. "I will check up on you later. It's really great to see you." She hugged Paige. Beverley took off in one direction and left Paige standing beside Colar.

Paige glanced around the room and could see that most of the people were from money. Some of them had not worked an honest day in their lives. She could also see from the looks of some of the guests that it was all about who had the most expensive things, and that was a huge turn-off for her.

As if reading her thoughts, Colar said, "I never like going to these events. If it were not for a good cause, I would not be here. But because I get to see you, it's worth enduring the phonies that are here tonight." He took her hand and tucked it in the crook of his arm. "Let's join the others."

Paige knees were shaking so hard that it was good Colar was holding her hand. The man's presence was wreaking havoc with her senses. It felt like a million butterfly wings were fluttering in her stomach. A low heat was beginning to simmer between her legs.

As they joined the others, Andy said, "You are beautiful,

Paige, and your gown is stunning. I can see Colar only has eyes for you."

"Yes," Gail said. "I don't think he has any intention of leaving your side tonight."

"Have you eaten yet?" Marche asked.

"No," Trista said.

"OK, great. Let's get something to eat." The girls grabbed plates, loaded them to overflowing, and found a place to sit and eat.

Colar was standing with his brothers and some of their former classmates, desperately trying to keep up with the conversation, but his eyes were following Paige everywhere she went. He was trying to maintain some distance from her, but the moment he'd seen her in that figure-hugging gown, his groin was enflamed. He knew that it would be better to avoid her for a while. He half-listened to what his companions were talking about, nodded where he was supposed to, and uttered a comment here and there.

Finally Christopher said through gritted teeth, "For God's sake, Colar. Why don't you just go and talk to her, instead of standing here salivating and lusting after her?"

Irritated that he was caught ogling Paige, Colar hissed his teeth. "Mind your damned business," he said as he strolled off.

Dandre' grinned as he said, "If you hurt her, your behind is mine."

"Yeah, whatever," Colar mumbled.

"What's wrong with him?" Chayse asked.

"Nothing, except he has a bad case of lust for Paige," Dandre' said.

"Yeah, tell me about it," Christopher replied.

Colar watched as Paige stuffed food in her mouth. He thought it was so sexy as her tongue darted out to lick her lips. The movement of her tongue caused heat to curl in the pit of his stomach. Unable to stay away, he strolled towards the table where Paige and the girls were sitting.

Several times he was stopped, and mostly by women. He could see that they were out in droves and on the prowl; most of them wore skimpy designer gowns and flashy jewellery. They were flocking to him. Any other time, Colar would have enjoyed the attention, but not tonight. He gritted his teeth in frustration at the grating voice of the female currently trying to hold his attention. She had been giving him a signal for weeks that she was readily available and looking for her next rich husband in order to keep the lifestyle to which she was accustomed. He was trying not to be insensitive or rude, but he could see that she was not getting the hint that he was uninterested. "I apologise," he said. "My mind was elsewhere." She batted he eyes and gave him a fake smile as she brushed his arms with her scantily clad breast. Her action left him cold. "I am sorry to disappoint you ladies, but tonight I am already spoken for," he said as he pulled away from the group.

"Oh, it's such a shame," the female in green purred. "Well, if you change your mind, you know where to find me."

Colar ignored the next group that tried to get his attention as he headed towards Paige. "Hi, are you having a good time?" he asked from behind her as he finally made his way to where she was standing. He grinned to himself when he saw her body stiffen for a moment and slowly turn to face him.

He felt his groin tighten and a clench in his gut as she looked at him with those incredible, exotic green eyes. Her face was stunning, and he could see the colour rising in her cheeks. As she blushed, he thought it was rather endearing and sweet to see a woman blush.

Paige looked at Colar like a deer caught in a headlight, momentarily at a loss for words. We was without a doubt the most gorgeous and sexy male she had encountered. His eyes were aquamarine blue with thick black lashes; they were stunningly beautiful. He had eyes that captivated and enticed. His jaw was chiselled, and he had a sensuous mouth with a dimple in his chin. He wore his long, blacker-than-midnight, glossy hair down his back. In contrast to that silky main, his smooth skin was tawny golden brown, which made a woman itch to feel his tall, powerful, muscular frame showcase the designer suit he wore. Yet there seem to be a certain lithe sensuality that in his movements. Like his brother Dandre', there was a captivating aura of individuality about him that gave the feeling this was a man who would do as he pleased.

Yet it was his face that captivated the most discriminating of women in the room. It was a face of utter masculine beauty and sensuality that made women gasp aloud. Simply put, he was breathtaking. His sensuous, full lips were tilted up in a smile that seemed to be hiding some deep, dark secret. His intense blue eyes regarded her as if she was a delicate morsel that he was about to gobble up.

"I am wonderful and yourself?" she finally managed to answer him.

"I am much better now that I am able to have you to myself,"

"Oh," Paige said breathlessly. "Why is that?" She couldn't figure out what he meant, but she found she was intrigued. She decided that just for tonight, she would let her hair down and have some fun, especially because she'd had a few glasses of champagne. Being on her guard around Colar was beginning to take its toll on her.

"May I have this dance?" Colar said as he held his hand out to her.

Paige stared at his outstretched hand for a moment before placing her hand in his and saying, "Sure." She was surprised by the nervous, quivering sensation in the pit of her stomach, which didn't seem to be subsiding. She could admit that she was dangerously attracted to him, but she could not figure out why he made her nervous.

Colar led her to the dance floor. As he pulled her close, she could feel the rapid beat of his heart, which seemed to mirror her own. She gazed into his eyes, which had a hypnotic effect on her. Paige felt like she was drowning in a sea of blue waters. As they moved to the music, Colar bent his head and whispered in her ear, "I want you, Paige."

"Haven't you heard? You don't always get what you want," she said with a smile. She knew she should make an excuse and get away from him as soon as the music stopped, but she found she was enjoying the flirting. What harm could be done, anyway? She would enjoy the moment. Tonight he was her prince, and she would be his Cinderella. When the clock stuck midnight, everything would be as it was before.

"Actually, no one has told me no since I was ten years old." He smiled. "I am the baby in the family, and so from my parents to my uncles, I always get what I want."

"Is that so? Well, Mr Neilson, I think it's time you are told that you can't have what you want," she said with a seductive smile. With that, she turned and walk off the dance floor.

Colar was rendered speechless for a moment. He stood there with his mouth gaping before he caught himself. He caught up with her as she slipped through the sliding glass door that led to the balcony.

She found she was turned on by his boldness. She leaned

over the railing of the balcony, desperately trying to catch her breath. Colar came up behind her and pressed himself against her. She could feel his manhood resting against the cheeks of her bottom. "What do you think you are doing?" she breathed.

"What does it feel like?" he said in a throaty, low, rich, melodious growl.

She glared at him, and as she slowly turned around, she could feel her pulse accelerating. She could tell by the look on his face that he could feel it too. Colar pulled her against his hard frame. Her eyes darkened with desire, and her breath came out against his neck in pants. He licked her ear and gently sucked the delicate skin of her neck. Desire began to flow through her core like a hot lava.

Paige trembled as he slid his arms around her and cupped her rounded bottom. Colar growled low in his throat, loving the feel of her as he allowed his hand to roam over the exposed portion of her back in a heated caress, leaving a trail of molten heat in the wake of his touch. Colar pulled back as he allowed his sensual, lambent blue eyes to roam over her face.

In a husky voice, he said, "You are beautiful." He lowered his head and captured her mouth in a hot kiss, engaging her tongue in a fiery duel. He licked and nipped on her bottom lip. Passion consumed him. Upon releasing her lip, Colar swiped his tongue across her cheek as he began raining butterfly kisses on the top of her nose, eyes, and forehead. The aggressive hunter within him met her motionless, captive look with a candid sensuality. At once, a languid veil of warmth surrounded her, followed by the exotic, heady smell of cardamom and nutmeg. His sexual scent surrounded her.

Paige pulled out of his embrace and said, "I should go. Besides, someone could see us."

Colar quickly grabbed a deck chair and pushed it under the doorknob. He did not want anyone interrupting his time with her. It had been a long time that he'd wanted to be with her, and no one was going to stop him.

Paige leaned against the railing and tried to get her body under control. She was playing a deadly game with a man who could eat her alive. "I really should go," she said barely above a whisper. She could not stop the shiver dancing up and down her spine.

"What's the hurry? Don't you like my company?" he asked in a sexy drawl. His hand continued to caress her arms, causing her body to shake with need. She was quickly losing her resolve to walk away. His naughty voice whispered, "Surely one night of recklessness would not hurt? Tell me you want me." His hands skimmed higher as he brushed the underside of her breasts, which were throbbing with longing for him to touch her nipples and were straining against her bra. The lace was irritating her sensitive skin.

She'd never wanted the touch of a man more than she did at this moment, more than her next breath. "No," she said.

"You are lying. Your lips are saying one thing, but your body is saying something else."

Paige opened her mouth to deny his words but found nothing came out. She could feel his erection as he pressed her close to his chest. She wrapped her arms around his neck as his hands roamed all over her body. She did not know how or when it happened, but she suddenly felt the warm breeze on her naked breast. In fiery passion, his mouth descended on her swollen breast. His lips were like silk and velvet. She could feel heat pooling in the centre of her feminine core. With one swift move, Colar slid down the zipper of her skirt. The garment made a rustling sound as it slid down her legs and pooled around her ankles. He used his hands to caress her stomach as he worked his way down to the waistband of her black lace thong.

Colar knelt before her as he inhaled her lush feminine scent. Using his teeth, he peeled the skimpy garment from her sex, covering her with his mouth and filling her with his taste, his scent, his velvet warmth. He was enticed, and he gave the kiss of a conqueror. Colar gently nudged her legs apart, his swift tongue dipping between her lips and shocking her into clutching his head to her as he stroked her insides, tasting her and swallowing her. He devoured her with an intensity. His tongue was as lethal as his fingers.

Paige whimpered deep in her throat. Sensations beyond her wildest dreams flooded her entire body. She began to shake as the first wave of ecstasy hit her, and she cried out as she held his head. His tongue increased its stroke, tasting her greedily while tremor after tremor raced through her body.

Her entire being shook with the pleasure he was giving her. Moments later when the tremors stopped and her body calmed down, Colar pulled up her skirt and fastened it. After standing up, he gently pulled her to him and embraced her tenderly, muttering in what sound like Italian. Paige had never experienced anything like this before. She had just experienced her first orgasm, and her body wanted more.

His arms went securely around her waist, bringing her snugly against him. After lowering his head, he began to suck on the skin of her neck and throat. "Come home and spend the night with me," he muttered. Paige could not speak and simply nodded in agreement. Colar took her by the hand as he gently led her down the stairs and outside to the parking lot.

On the drive to his home, neither of them spoke. Paige

closed her eyes as she listened to the smooth, sultry sound of reggae that emanated from the sound system in the car.

Upon entering his home, Colar led Paige to his bedroom. His body was on fire, but he knew he had to take it slow. He was aware that she was inexperienced—not that it mattered. He smile at the thought that he was the first to introduce her to the world of ecstasy.

Paige felt like she was in a trance as Colar removed both their clothes. His movements were graceful and sophisticated, like an artist. His velvet lips touched her shoulder in a feather-light kiss as he used his hands to undo the clasp that held up her hair. Colar ran his fingers through her hair as he watched the red strands flow over his hands in gentle waves. With strong arms, he scooped her up and walked over to the bed, tossing back the covers. He gently laid her down. Her eyes fluttered open as she watched him join her. He bent his head as he captured her luscious lips. As he kissed her neck, he worked his way down to her breasts. His hands rubbed along her thighs, and she wanted more. She needed him in a way she had never needed a man before.

His hands brushed over the curls at the junction of her thighs. He almost lost all sense of control when he felt her wetness. She was the most responsive woman he had ever been with, and there was nothing fake about her. She was all woman and was writhing in pleasure beneath him. He buried his head between her legs, and her sweet scent hit him. He felt his body throb with painful desire. He made a low, husky sound as he used his tongue to stroke her clitoris. Paige was driving him crazy with purring sounds.

Colar forced his way between her legs. She could feel him against her; the broad head of his thick, enormous shaft was at the entrance of her feminine core. In one swift, powerful thrust, he pierced her, breaking through the barrier. Paige screamed as she felt the pain, making her aware that he was deeply embedded in her to the hilt, stretching her. She kept her eyes tightly shut.

"Open your eyes, sweetheart," he said. "I want you to look at me. Are you OK? Do you want me to stop?"

"No," Paige whispered. She opened her eyes slowly, and luminous green pools gazed up at him. He began to move. He withdrew halfway and slid into her. She gasped. "Ooh, my. Please."

He made a low, husky sound against her as he established a steady rhythm. His scent engulfed her, making her dizzy with desire. He licked her neck and throat. As he kissed her, they were engaged in a dance as old as time. She made little purring sounds. As the sensation intensified, he acknowledge them by nipping her earlobe. Each thrust became more powerful than the last. She bit his shoulders to stop herself from screaming.

He was a raging storm. The tempest of his sexual appetites called forth her latent passion. Paige wrapped her legs around his waist as the fire built within her. She could feel herself spiralling out of control, and she couldn't breathe. Paige screamed as the first orgasm ripped through her. Wave upon wave of pleasure flowed through her, and she arched her back as Colar increased the rhythm. She felt him begin to pulse in her, which triggered another orgasm. He tightened his hold on her as her body begin to milk him. At that moment, Colar threw his head back and released his seed deep into her womb with a final thrust that nearly lifted her off the bed. He growled and collapsed on her. Colar thought he would have died from the intensity of the pleasure he'd just experience in Paige's arms.

After they had made love two more times, he cuddled her in his arms. She watched him silently, her lips gently parted. There was wonder on her face as she drifted off to sleep.

Paige woke up in the wee hours of the morning. She started to panic because she did not know where she was. As she moved and felt arms around her, memories came flooding her mind. As she moved, she felt the soreness between her legs. Paige slowly untangled herself from his embrace, and he started to stir. She went completely still. She wanted nothing more than to get as far away from him as possible. She finally untangled herself, got out of bed, and looked for her clothes. She quickly dressed and walked out the door.

Colar woke up some time later, after Paige had slipped away. After looking around in disbelief, he could not believe she had left. He sighed in frustration as he dragged his fingers through his hair. No woman had ever left his bed before. He was usually the one doing the leaving. This did not sit well with him at all. A part of him wanted to go find her and drag her back to bed.

CHAPTER 9

Working at a family-owned business has its rewards, Andy mused as she sat at her desk. She had the opportunity to design buildings, houses, and highways. She loved her job and never ceased to be amazed at the thrill she experienced at the completion of one of her creations.

The hospital that she had designed was now completed. The new, state-of-the-art cardiac unit was everything a cardiologist could dream of. In a few days, the grand opening was scheduled to take place. Mr Crosby was pleased with himself because the unit would be named after his late wife, Edna Crosby. The entire staff was invited to the grand opening. Like her, they were excited to see the finished product of their hard labour. There was something about cutting ribbons and popping champagne corks at a new building; it gave the feeling of Christmas.

The phone rang. Chuckling to herself, Andy lifted the receiver. "Hello?"

On the other end of the line was her mother. "OK, Mommy, slow down. I can't understand what you are saying."

Anita was crying so hard, and in between sobs she said, "It's Melody. She was in a car accident this morning."

"All right, Mom." I am on my way."

It took forty-five minutes for Andy to reach the hospital,

and already it was crowded with Neilson and Spencer family members. Andy walked over to her father, hugged him, and asked what had happened. Her father replied, "Melody's car was hit by a drunk driver."

"At this time of the morning?" bellowed Chayse. "It is not even twelve o'clock! What idiot starts dinking this early?"

"Calm down, son," Colee'rt said. "Everything is going to be all right."

"How is she doing? Any word about her condition yet?"

"No," Christopher replied. "They have taken her to surgery." He went back to pacing the floor.

"Come sit by me, dear," Grace, Melody's mom, said as she watched her son-in-law with concern. Sighing, Christopher walked over to the couch where his mother-in-law was sitting. No sooner had he sat down than he jumped back up again, unable to sit still.

Dandre' looked at his brother and could see the worry etched all over his face. Not only was his brother worried about his wife, but he was also worried about their unborn child. In an attempt to divert his brother, Dandre' suggested that they go to the cafeteria to get coffee. His mother shook her head no. "You guys go. We will stay here." The men pulled Christopher out of the room and walked him to the café to get some much-needed coffee. None of them said anything; they simply drank their coffee and let the ladies have some time together.

When enough time had passed, they finally made their way back to the waiting room with coffee and donuts to share. The women managed to get Melody's mom, Grace, to drink some coffee, but no amount of pleading could get her to eat.

The hours waiting for the doctors to come out were the longest of Christopher's life. He paced up and down the hallways, waiting for any news. He needed to know that his wife and child were going to be all right.

"Mr Neilson?" a doctor said as he stepped into the room.

Christopher looked at the doctor with both fear and hope. Nothing could have happened to Melody; she was his life, and he would not survived without her. "Yes?" he said in a gruff voice. He was terrified but needed to know.

"Your wife is out of surgery. However, she is unconscious. The next few hours are critical."

"What about the baby?" he asked.

"For now, everything seem to be OK with the baby. Your wife's concussion is severe, however there seem to be no permanent brain damage so far. There is no dangerous swelling inside the skull. She may come out of it in a few hours, or it could take days or even weeks."

Tears rose in the grey pools of Christopher's eyes before he turned his head away. His nostrils flared as he breathed deep in an effort to control his emotions. "Thanks, Doctor. I am so damn glad to know something, I thought maybe they didn't make it, and no one wanted to tell me. Can I see her?"

"Only for a few minutes. I suggest that all of you don't go in at the same time."

"We understand, Doctor," Karl, Melody's father, said. He turned to Christopher. "I think you should go first, son."

Christopher hovered over the bed where his wife lay motionless. He was grossly pale, and his eyes were moist. His tousled hair hung over his face as he used the back of his hand to caress her face. He muttered in broken French phrases, letting her know that he loved her and would be there for her.

After Christopher came out, Andy, Dandre', and their parents went in to see Melody. They stood in silence, watching the slow rise and fall of her chest. Andy caught herself studying the swollen contours of Melody abdomen. *It's a miracle that her child is still nestled safely in her womb.* She wondered how the baby was faring and whether Melody knew somehow that the new life inside her was safe, at least for now. It would be a very beautiful baby if it resembled its mother, but especially if it shared the genes of both parents.

Sometime later, the nurse came in and advised them, "It's time to leave so Melody can get her rest." Christopher had a different idea. After some coaxing, they were able to get him to leave. The nurse had advised that he could come back later to see her during visiting hours.

As the two families left the ward and proceeded through the corridors that led to the elevators, no one said a word. Each person was in his or her own little world, wondering whether Melody would pull through. They silently emerged from the building and proceeded across the courtyard to their vehicles.

Camera flashes went off. Television lights came on in a white-hot blaze as cameras swung in their direction, and news anchors smoothed their hair and ran towards them. Within seconds, they were surrounded.

Dandre' swore in French as he pulled Andy close to his side, thrusting an arm out before him. He set his face with a hard look and shoved through the shouting mob. At the parking lot, he opened the passenger door of his Jaguar and hefted Andy inside with more strength than finesse. He glanced over his shoulder and could see the rest of the family making a beeline for their cars. Dandre' hurried inside the car, clicked his seat belt, and set the powerful car in motion, peeling away with a shriek of rubber while the paparazzi dove for safety on the other side.

Andy fastened her seat belt with shaking hands, and she

glanced behind them. "They are following us," she said in a breathless whisper.

Dandre's only reply was to floor the accelerator. They zoomed out of the parking lot and screeched on to a busy street, to the blast of horns and squeaking brakes. Then they sped away into the sunbathed afternoon. Driving liked a maniac, he took out his cell phone and dialled his parents' number, telling them how to lose the press and make a clean get away.

After a few moments, Andy said, "I wonder how the media got wind of the accident so soon. I almost forget that Melody father is running for governor."

Dandre' said, "Yeah, when you are in the public eye, there is no privacy."

Andy soon lost track of the many turns they made or the streets they took while staying ahead of the press. They drove through an old section of the city, taking back roads and alleys in an effort to ditch the paparazzi. Moments later, they were on the other side of town. Dandre' glanced in his rear-view mirror to see whether they were being followed. He pulled into an underground garage, turned off the ignition, looked at Andy, and said, "Sorry, my heart. I did not mean to scare you."

"I know," she said. "What are we doing here?"

"I am changing cars."

"Oh. I left my car at the hospital."

"Don't worry about it. We will collect it later."

"Where are?" Did we lose them?"

Dandre' replied, "Wait."

She heard it then: the sound of vehicles roaring past on the street beyond the building. A few moments longer and the pursuit died away in the distance.

She said, "I know we can't avoid them forever. Christopher's or Melody's parents need to make a statement. Under the circumstances, I don't know what else your family could have done."

Dandre' smiles and said, "Oh, a number of things, such as setting up decoys, taking the limo, and putting security guards in place."

"Do you think Melody and the baby are going to be all right?"

"Yes, they have to be. If not, my brother will not make it." A small cry came from Andy's mouth. He pulled her into his arms. "Please don't cry. Everything will be fine. Besides, Christopher has all of us. He won't have to go through this alone. Melody is getting the best care possible. I will speak to my father about having security posted at the hospital."

"I know. It just seems so unfair that because of some fool, she is lying in a hospital unconscious and fighting for her life and the life of her child."

He said, "Before the excitement, I thought we could stop for some lunch on the way back to the house."

"You are hungry?"

"Yes. What can I say? Being chased does that to me," he said with a gleam in his eyes.

Andy gave him a quick glance. Then with a smile of her own, she decided to ignore the suggestion beneath his words. Instead, she asked, "Are you sure we won't be ambushed again?"

"I will do my best to make sure it doesn't happen."

She leaned back in her seat and ran nervous fingers through her hair. From the corner of his eye, Dandre' saw how nervous she was. He reached over and gave her hand a gentle squeeze. Andy was grateful for his silent strength at a time when all hell was breaking loose. She drew comfort and strength from him with the reassurance that everything would be all right. Andy silently prayed that Melody would pull through and that her niece or nephew would be OK.

"Stopping for lunch really isn't necessary," she said as the city began to fade away behind them. "We could go back to your place and have Ettie give us a sandwich or something."

Dandre' gave her a swift look, narrowing his eyes against the strong wind that swirled around them. "I prefer something heartier," he replied. "Besides, I thought you need a moment to relax and forget about everything for a little while. It's my duty to feed you, I suppose." He grinned. "You are pale and shaking, mon cheri. You're probably more shaken by what took place back there than you realise. Some small diversion should be useful as well as pleasant."

The knowledge that he paid attention to her appearance warmed her heart. "OK," she said with a giggle. "Only for a little while."

"Come closer and lay your head on my shoulder. Close your eyes and rest. I will wake you when we get there." Andy sighed and did as he said. Surprisingly, she slept the smooth movement of the car, and Dandre's nearness lulled her to sleep.

When she opened her eyes, she yawned and asked, "Where are we?"

"Sugar Bay," he drawled in a lazy voice. The building overlooking the sea had a rustic and inviting look, with its façade of light blue weathered wood. The red and blue awning flapped lazily in the gentle breeze.

After stepping from the car with Dandre's assistance, Andy realised she was indeed hungry. The scent of seafood mixed with the spicy aroma of jerk chicken was enough to awaken her taste buds and cause her mouth to water.

Upon entering the establishment, they were greeted by a petite woman with a white apron fastened around her tiny waist. She gave Dandre' a warm hug and scolded him for not visiting her more often. "Come," she said, leading them towards the back of the restaurant. She eyed Andy with open curiosity as she retreated towards the kitchen.

Dandre' ordered a bottle of house wine, and warm, hard dough bread with butter appeared with the wine. The waitress poured a little of the wine in a glass for Dandre' to taste, got for his approval, and filled Andy's glass first. The waitress recited the menu in the local Patwa dialect. After taking their order, she asked in a flirtatious voice if there was anything else, looking at Dandre'.

He took Andy's hand in his and said, "No, thanks. My fiancée and I are OK."

The waitress gave Andy a venomous look as she walked away.

Andy sighed, leaned back in her chair, and said, "I can't blame her for trying. You are breathtaking."

Chuckling, Dandre' said, "I suppose so, but I have all the woman I want sitting here with me." Leaning back at a slight angle, Dandre' stretched his long, lean legs, crossed them at the ankles, and picked up his glass of wine. As his gaze roamed over her face, she could see the hot desire simmering in their golden depths. In a husky voice, he said, "To me, you are the most beautiful woman on the planet, Anjou. You complete me."

A fierce heat pooled between her legs as his melodious voice washed over her. She took a deep breath and said, "You, my prince, are my world. I can't wait to be your wife."

Before Dandre' could respond, the waitress returned and placed two steaming plates before them, shattering the moment of intimacy.

"Eat, drink your wine, and relax, mon cheri. We will finish this later," he said as he winked at her.

"It is so beautiful here, so quiet and peaceful." The only sound was the sound of the sea, as well as the clatter of pots, pans, and dishes in the kitchen as the chef prepared meals for the patrons. Andy sipped her wine, and a languid feeling began to seep over her. Whether it was the food, the wine, the cook, the beauty of the day, or the place, it seemed to Andy that she had never tasted such delicious food.

Before she knew it, her plate was empty, and so was the wine bottle. After wiping her mouth with her napkin, she looked at Dandre' and sent him a very heated message, which he understood. She could tell by the dilating of his pupils, and his gaze drifted slowly from her mouth to her breasts under her silk blouse and back again.

Dandre' rose slowly to his feet after tossing enough money on the table to cover the cost and a tip for their waitress. He stretched out his hand to her. "Shall we, Ms Royale?"

When they reached the car, Dandre' pulled Andy into his arms and devoured her mouth. His kisses were hot and feverish, mirroring her desire for him. Andy made a purring sound that gave him more access to her mouth. He sucked her tongue and licked her lips. "Mmm, delicious," he said, taking her bottom lip between his teeth as he nipped it with just enough pressure to create a sting but leaving in its wake a pleasurable feeling. He stepped back and brushed her cheeks with his hand.

The day was getting hot. Andy removed her jacket before getting in the car. Dandre' leaned over to snap her seat belt in place. By leaning forward, she rubbed her breast against his cheeks. Growling deep in his throat, Dandre' straightened and said, "You, my beautiful enchantress, are going to be the death of me."

She stared into his lambent eyes with a coy smile on her face before saying, "Who, me?"

"Ah, I see you like to play, mon cheri, but I promise you will pay for this later!"

"Oh, is that a threat?"

"No, it's a promise," he said, closing the door as he got behind the wheel.

Dandre' left the restaurant behind, drove to a nearby town, pulled the car into a secluded area, and cut the engine. He turned towards Andy and said, "I have an uncontrollable desire to have you on my lap."

With a saucy smile, she replied, "That can be arranged."

Before she could take her next breath, he leaned to slide an arm around her waist. The console was in the way, but he hardly noticed. He grabbed her head and wrapped her hair around his hand as he pulled her to him. She made a soft sound as he captured her mouth with his. He could not get enough of her.

Dandre' released her mouth and removed his hand from her hair long enough to adjust his seat. Once that was done, he effortlessly lifted Andy onto his lap with her back to the steering wheel as she straddled him. After unbuttoning her blouse with a flick of wrist, he released the clasp of her bra. He took one pert breast in his mouth and licked and sucked to his heart's content. His breath was becoming laboured. Dandre' pushed her skirt high to her waist, as he used his hand to ease her thong out of the way. Her lush scent caused his nostrils to flare, and he inserted his finger inside. She was wet and tight. At touch of his finger, Andy began to writhe, making a whimpering sound in her throat at the intense pleasure he gave her body. She shivered at his intimate touch. Andy closed her eyes as she concentrated on what he was doing to her. He establish a rhythm that made her quiver. Andy felt like she was going to die. Her breath became shaky as she opened her legs wider. Everything around her was spinning out of control as an orgasm of gigantic proportions slammed through her, and she screamed.

Dandre' almost lost it as Andy screamed. He released his zipper and was hard as a rock. He lifted her on his erection, and with one swift thrust, he was buried deep inside her body. Each time he thrust into her, his neck strained. He held her gaze, forcing her to look at him each time he thrust into her body. Dandre' knew he was acting like a randy, horny teenager, but he did not care. This woman who was riding him made him lose all control every time he was around her. No other woman had ever affected him the way Anjou did. Like her name, she was sweeter than wine. He was intoxicated with her, inflamed with his love for her.

Throwing her head back, Andy screamed as an orgasm ripped through her. "Dandre', oh, Dandre'1" was all she could say as her legs quivered from the aftermath of her release.

He captured her lips in a deep kiss as he surrendered to his own release. Gasping for breath, he wrapped his arms around her. She lay limply against his chest. "That was incredible," he said as he kissed her on the head. "I love you so much, Anjou, and I can't wait to be your husband."

Andy was at a loss for words and was content to bask in the afterglow of their lovemaking as she listened to the strong beat of his heart. Andy glanced at the man sitting beside her, at the beautiful, stern planes of his face, the golden eyes that narrowed, and the wind that ruffled his hair. He drove with single-minded concentration yet an expansive air, as if the road had been designed for his use alone. The blood of Greek and French nobles flowed through his veins, and it was displayed in his masculine features. He was self-assured to the point of arrogance, and he had an air of certainty that he knew what was best for everyone around him. No man had ever affected her the way he did.

CHAPTER 10

It was almost six weeks since Melody's accident, and Andy was still very tense, although Melody was out of danger. Trista, Gail, Marconnets, Marche, and Paige stormed into Andy's her office.

"Get your handbag, Andy. Let's go. We are not taking no for an answer."

"Where are we going?" Andy asked.

"We are going for a much-needed day of pampering," Marche said.

"I can't leave. I have a lot to do," she pleaded."

"Heifer, don't make me hurt you. You own the company, for god's sake!" Paige said. "You can either walk out with us, or we will get your brother to come and drag you out. One way or the other, you are coming with us."

"OK, OK. I guess it wouldn't hurt to get out for a few hours," Andy conceded. The women nodded encouragingly. She gathered her handbag and made sure her computer was powered down before reluctantly following the women from the room.

"First we are going to get some lunch," Gail said.

"Then we are going to the salon for manicures and pedicures," Marche added. "After all that fun, we are going shopping—and don't you dare argue with us."

Andy sighed and said, "Shopping? The wedding is just weeks away. I should get some new lingerie for my honeymoon."

"Do you know where you are going?" Trista asked.

"No. Dandre' wants to keep it a surprise."

The six women ate an amazing lunch, which had Paige groaning and wishing she could unbutton her pants. On the way to the salon, Andy realised they had not had a girl's night out in six weeks.

"We know you are worried about Melody," Marche said. "But you must believe she and the baby will be all right. She will be well taken care of. Besides, Christopher has round-the-clock medical care for her."

"I know. It's just the thought that she could have died or lost the baby because of some drunk. I think we should stop by the house to see her."

"That is a great idea. Melody is like a bear with a sore head. I can't imagine what that must be like for her. I spoke with her on the phone a few days ago," Marconnets said. "The poor darling is going out of her mind with having to be still. She tried to bribe Christopher to have her assistant bring some work from the office."

"What was Christopher's response?" Trista asked, giggling.

Marconnets said, "His response was absolutely not."

"Then it's settled," Gail said. "We will pay her a visit. It will do her some good to see our friendly faces, considering she is on bed rest."

"Yes," replied Marconnets. "Doctor's order. Poor thing—that has to be hard on her."

Andy ran her hands along the silk of some gowns and knew that she have to get them. The ladies squealed with delight, and by the end of their shopping, she was glad that she had taken the time off. She didn't know how they had managed it, but they were leaving the store with several bags. By the time they headed to her brother-in-law's house, Andy realised she'd had an amazing day.

Melody was delighted to see the ladies. Christopher, who was hovering over her, was shooed away by the ladies. "Such undying devotion," Marconnets teased, rolling his eyes.

Chris realised he had no choice but to leave. "I am fine, dear," Melody said. "You can stop fussing over me."

"I'm just worried about you. After all, you were in a terrible accident," Chris said as he kissed her on the lips.

Melody had been in a dreadful mood the last couple of days and was very sick of lying in bed. She had always been very active and was thoroughly sick of bed rest.

Chris said, "Remember, Dr Morgan said you can't overdo it—only light walks, and no work for at least another four weeks."

"How could I forget when I have you to remind me, sweetheart?" Melody said with a smile on her face.

"I love you so much, Mel," he said. "If I had lost you, I would have died too. I can't imagine my life without you."

"I love you too, Christopher. Now, go relax for a while. I promise I will not vanish into thin air. Besides I would love to chat with these ladies."

Before long, the girls had Melody doubling over with laughter. Gail was hilarious as she told them of the tricks she used to play on the nuns at the all-girls Catholic school she'd attended. The Mother Superior had threatened so many times to have her expelled if she did not behave herself. The only saving grace was her grades exceeded expectations, and her parents were very big givers to the school.

Dandre' strolled into the Half-Moon Hotel to attend the annual governor's ball that the constituencies hosted each year for charity. He walked farther into the elegantly decorated ball room and immediately began searching for Anjou. Laser-sharp eyes took a cursory inspection of the multitude of linen-covered tables and the shining marble floor with gleaming chandeliers hanging from vaulted ceiling. He searched for the most beautiful woman in the room who happened to be the object of his desires.

Finally, he spotted her talking with his brothers; they were standing at the far corner of the room, and she was laughing at something Chayse had said. She was wearing a royal blue evening gown with a deep vee that left her back bare and a tantalizing split that showcased her gorgeous legs. She looked good to eat, and to say he was hungry for her was an understatement. When it came to Anjou, his appetite was ravenous. He gave a wolfish grin and made his way towards his lady.

Colar spotted him first. Dandre' motioned with his finger to not say anything. He walked up behind her and wrapped his arms around her waist. "Hello, beautiful," he purred sensuously in her ear.

"Dandre'!" She turned around and wrapped her arms around his neck.

He chuckled at her enthusiasm. "That's the welcome I was hoping to receive."

"When did you get back?" she asked.

"A few hours ago. My business concluded earlier than expected, so here I am. I did try to call you, but your phone was off.

"I am sorry," Andy said. "But you are here now, and I am very happy to see –"

Before she could finish her sentence, Dandre' captured her lips in a hot kiss.

He finally released her when Christopher cleared his throat. "Well, hello to you too, brother," Chris said, chuckling.

"Hi, guys. How are you doing?" Dandre' asked.

"I am glad you made it," Colar said.

"Me too," he replied. He released her waist and took her hand as Gail, Trista, Paige, Marconnets, and Marche joined them.

"Have you eaten?" they enquired.

"No," Andy said.

"OK, let's grab something to eat."

Just before Dandre' release her hand, he brought it to his mouth and placed a tender kiss in the middle of her palm. "Hurry back," he said in a husky voice.

"Damn, you got it bad," Colar said as he watched Dandre's eyes follow Andy while she walked away with the others.

"Yes, I do," he replied. "I can't wait to marry that woman."

"I know how you feel," Christopher said. "I share your sentiment."

"We are happy for you both," Chayse and Colar said, "but we're never falling in love or getting married."

"Oh, you will," Dandre' said with a grin.

"So now you are a prophet? You can predict our future?" Chayse replied.

"Just keep on living, little brother. You will see there is a woman out there somewhere who is going to capture your heart real soon."

"Whatever," Colar said, hissing his teeth as he walked away.

Later on that evening, as Dandre' danced with Andy, he felt someone tap him on the shoulders. He turned around and saw Melody's father, Governor Spencer. "Sorry for the interruption, son, but I need to ask a favour. One of our bachelors is unable to make it. Can you replace him in the auction tonight?"

Dandre' looked at Andy before turning his attention to the governor. "I am sorry, sir, but I don't think I can."

Andy touched his arm. "It's OK, honey. It's for a great cause—and I will bid on you."

"Are you sure?" he asked.

"Yes, I am," she replied.

"Then it's settled," the governor said, smiling at her. "I am forever in you debt." He soon walked away.

Dandre' wrapped his arms around Andy and gave her a sensuous kiss before walking to the stage.

"Ladies," the master of ceremonies said, "the time that you have patiently waited for has arrived. All proceeds with go to the Leukemia Foundation, so please be generous with your bidding!" He motioned to the men, and each stepped forward and introduced himself before stepping back. "Without further ado, ladies, please get your bids in. The winner will be announced within the hour!"

"Did you bid on me?" Dandre' asked as he led Andy on the dance floor later on.

"Why, yes, of course," she replied. "Are you kidding me? No one is leaving here with you tonight."

"Is that so?" Dandre' said.

"I have very big plans for you tonight, Mr Neilson."

"I can't wait," he said, chuckling as he pulled her into his arms.

One dance turned into four, and they were oblivious to

everything and everyone around them as they focused on each other. The need to taste her was overwhelming. He lowered his head and used his teeth to nip her earlobe. Her arms encircled his neck, and his scent was driving her crazy. Andy purred deep in her throat as she felt his teeth on her ear. A shiver danced up and down her spine.

Just then, Dandre' was called back to the stage. "Is it an hour already?" she wondered. She reluctantly released her arms from around his neck as he stepped back and walked towards the stage.

"OK, ladies and gentlemen. All the bids are in, and we will start with the highest bidder. Ms Anjou Royal has placed the highest bid for the night and won the pleasure of Mr Dandre' Neilson's company for the evening." He glanced into the audience and waved his hand invitingly. "Come on up and claim your date, Ms Royale."

Andy glided gracefully across the room, stepped on the podium, and linked her arms with Dandre', escorting him from the stage.

"How much did you bid?" Dandre' asked, his interest piqued.

Grinning like the cat that swallowed the canary, she replied, "That's for me to know and you to find out." She winked with a coy smile.

"Oh, so it's like that, huh?" Dandre' said, shaking his head at her.

"Well, I had to bid to ensure that no one else outbid me," she said. "Besides, I have huge plans for you tonight."

"Well, Ms Royale, I am all yours. What would you like to do?"

She wrapped her arms around his neck and said, "Let's get out of here."

"It would be my pleasure to oblige the missus," he said with a grin.

It was a perfect day for a barbeque. The morning sun rose clear and bright. Andy stepped out on the veranda, closing her eyes as she took a deep breath. The morning air was crisp and fresh. She wrapped her arms around herself and sighed in contentment. A feeling of excitement bubbled up within her. In a little while, the Neilsons' backyard would be a beehive of activity as the long-awaited family barbeque got underway. The entire Neilson clan would be there, and so would hers. There was her father, Colee'rt; mother, Anita; grandmother, Lila; brothers and sister, Paige, Gail, Trista, Tyler, and Jonas; and administrative assistant, Mrs Gray.

Paige was sitting on a padded bench and bouncing Marcus, her godson on her knees. Colar straddled the bench behind her, sitting until he was pressed against her. She could feel his erection pressing against her backside. He reached around her and touched Marcus's hands while whispering in her ears, "You are avoiding me. You can run, Paige dear, but you can't hide."

"Is that so?" she asked.

"Yes, it is so. You see, I have put my mark on you."

Before she could reply, Grandma Nadia walked over. "You are very good with him, dear." Paige looked up as Grandma Nadia smiled at her before glancing whimsically at her grandson. "Maybe one day …" Her words trailed off.

Tyler sighed as Melody, who was sitting beside Christopher, hid a smile behind her hand.

"Ha, thank you." Paige smiled nervously, suddenly feeling that without her knowledge, she was being auditioned to be the next granddaughter-in-law.

"You will make a wonderful mother, dear," Grandma Nadia predicted, her attention still trained on Paige. "Have you ever thought of settling down?"

"Um, well, I …" Paige swallowed hard.

"Oh, Grandma," Colar said with a sigh. "Please leave Paige alone."

Nadia glanced innocently from Paige to her grandson. "What did I do?"

"You are kidding me, right, Grandma?" Colar said, chuckling.

Before Grandma Nadia could answer, Paige said, "I think I should take him inside." She made a hasty retreat.

Sometime later, Paige wondered whether Grandma Nadia knew something. She had made an appointment to see her ob-gyn because she was late for her period. Not wanting to think about it anymore, she went in search of the others. Colar's words rang in her ears as she walked across the patio to where Andy was standing: "I have put my mark on you." *What the hell is that supposed to mean?*

The smell of jerk pork, fried chicken, roast fish, grilled lobster, and barbeque ribs filled the atmosphere in the Neilsons' backyard. It was seventy-nine degree, and a light wind blew over the island. The birds were singing sweetly in the trees overhead. Dandre' whistled as he manned the grill.

His father came to stand beside him. "Son, everything smells so wonderful. You're doing a great job."

"Thanks, Dad. I learned from the best."

Juan Neilson chuckled and took a sip of his guava punch. The older man was a replica of his sons. He was tall with broad, muscular shoulders. At fifty-eight, his dark hair was slightly greying at his temples. "You were humming. I take it that you are happy?"

"Yes, I am very happy. Now I understand what you meant when you told me you can't live without Mom."

"Your mother is my life. I love her more today than when I first met her. I believe finding true love is once in a lifetime, but sometimes when you are young, you are inclined to make foolish mistakes that could cost you that love. If a man is really lucky, he may experience it again, but there are no guarantees. When that opportunity comes along, you should grasp it with both hands and embrace it with all of your heart. There is no greater feeling than sharing your life with someone you love and being loved by that special person in return.

"Marriage is not a bed of roses, son. Even the most beautiful roses have thorns that can prick you. Just like everything in life, there are ups and downs in marriage. But if you are diligent, you can find the solution to any marital issues you may encounter." After patting Dandre' on the back, Juan said, "I think I'll go see if your mother needs some help with the potato salad." He winked at Chayse as he strutted away.

Sometime later, Paige stopped by the kitchen to check on Andy and the girls, who were helping with the food preparation. She took a few minutes to compose herself before rejoining the rest of the guest. She was halfway in the room when she spotted Grandma Nadia removing some ginger from the refrigerator.

"Did Marcus settle in?" Nadia asked without turning around.

After taking a deep breath, Paige entered the kitchen. "Yes. That little darling is out like a light," she said.

"Children can be such a delight," Nadia said.

"Yes, they can be."

"I am happy we have a moment alone," Nadia said, turning to face her. "I hope I didn't embarrass you earlier, dear."

"No, of course not," Paige said, lying through her teeth with a smile.

"Are you sure?" At Paige's nod, Nadia chuckled and said, "I am glad. My grandson Chayse wants ginger beer, so I came in to make it for him."

"Oh," Paige said, heaving a silent sight of relief and glad for the subject change.

Nadia gave a knowing look. "He is wonderful, don't you think? All my grandsons are wonderful, to tell the truth. I think they are spoilt rotten, especially that Colar."

Paige was surprised to hear Nadia acknowledge that her grandsons were spoilt. Not wanting the focus to return to her and Colar, she quickly said, "Grandma Nadia, will you show me how to make the ginger beer?"

"Why, of course, dear. I would be delighted to show you."

Dandre' entered the kitchen and walked over to where Andy was standing by the stove, stirring a big pot of Callaloo. "Mmm, that smells so good," he said, wrapping his arms around her waist.

Andy leaned into him as he nuzzled her neck. "I missed you," she said in a throaty whisper. She could feel her body responding to his nearness, and she turned around and wrapped her arms around his neck. "I can't wait to have you to myself later," she breathed as he gently licked her lips with his tongue.

"You two should get a room," Colar said as he and Christopher walked into the kitchen, chuckling.

Dandre' said, "Don't tempt me." He released Andy and stepped back. "I'd better go. I don't want to burn the meat on the grill. I will see you later."

"OK, see you later," Andy said.

Drusilla, Dandre's mom, walked over. "Anjou, dear, I am about to make the pound cake. Would you like to assist me?"

"Oh, sure," Andy replied. "Besides, I have to learn your secret! I know pound cake is Dandre's favourite, and if I can get mine to taste half as good as yours, then I would be very happy."

Drusilla took her hand and led her over to the mixing bowl. "You mix, and I will add ingredients." Anjou turned on the mixer, and Dru began adding ingredients. "We start by creaming a pound of butter at room temperature. Then we will add three cups of sugar until smooth. Then we will add six eggs, one at a time, blending each one well. I will add two shots of brandy to give it a little kick." She laughed at the horrified look on Andy's face. "I know the ingredients are sinfully rich, but we old-schoolers cook for fun and with a lot of love, not by counting calories."

"You are right. Nothing tastes as delicious as your traditional recipes. Besides, we don't eat like this every day. We all need to indulge or splurge every once in a while."

"Amen," Drusilla said. "Then I will add some lemon extract into the bowl. Next, we will add two and a half cups of flour. You see, this is a very simple recipe. While you are blending, I will prepare the baking pan."

A short while later, Andy poured the batter into the baking pan. "We will set the oven at 350 degrees and bake for forty-five minutes," Drusilla said.

Sighing, Andy said, "I remembered being in the kitchen with my mom while growing up."

"Yes, dear. She mentioned it earlier. I can see where you get your love for cooking."

"I enjoyed those times with her."

"She did as much as you do," Dru said.

Andy laughed and said, "I was more trouble underfoot than being a help. I remember having more ingredients in my hair than in the bowl. Thank you for showing me how to make it."

"You are very welcome, my dear." Drusilla kissed her cheeks.

CHAPTER 11

"What are my two favourite ladies up to?" Dandre' said, strolling into the kitchen.

At the sight of him, Andy's eyes lit up.

"Are you finished grilling?" Drusilla asked while giving her son a hug.

"Yes, I am for now," he replied. "While I was grilling, what were you two doing?"

"Oh, talking and baking. Your mom showed me how to make your favourite pound cake."

"Did she, now?"

"And what is that supposed to mean, Dandre' Roland Neilson?" his mother asked, placing her hand on her hips with an indignant look on her face.

"Relax, Mom. I just wondered if I should be concerned. I thought perhaps you told her some of my deep, dark secret." He chuckled.

"Now, why would you be concerned?" Drusilla said.

"Everything is fine," Andy said, saving him from answering.

"You said she showed you how to make pound cake?" His eyes lit up as a big grin appeared on his face. "Anjou, wait until you taste it. It's twelve hundred calories, but Lord, it's so worth it. Mom, do you think you could make a pound cake just for me at my wedding? Heaven knows I don't need the extra calories, but nothing is going to keep me from that cake."

Smiling, Drusilla said, "I hope you won't be disappointed."

"Come on, Mom. You know you are the best," Dandre' said.

"You are prejudiced towards me because I am your mother." She laughed.

After kissing his mother's cheeks, Dandre' turned to Andy, "Are you done in here?"

Drusilla said, "Go ahead, dear. I will be right out once I finish cleaning up."

"OK," Andy said. She took Dandre's arm as they walked into the backyard.

"It seems like you were having a good time with my mother," Dandre' said to Andy.

"Your mother is wonderful. Being with her brought back childhood memories," Andy said, chuckling. She walked over to sit beside Marche and Trista, who were sitting at a picnic table under a guava tree near the grill.

Dandre' released her hand and placed a light kiss on her mouth before joining Christopher at the grill.

"How are things going in the kitchen?" Trista asked.

"Great Grandma Nadia is making her famous ginger beer. We are in for a treat. The women of this family are great cooks."

The barbeque ended rather early because Melody's water broke, and Christopher rushed her to the hospital. Dandre' glanced at Chayse before saying, "Looks like there is going to be a new Neilson born tonight."

It didn't take long for Dandre' and Andy to get to the

hospital, and already it was crowded with Neilsons and Spencers. If anyone was curious why there were so many of them, no one mentioned it. It was almost 6.00 p.m., and everyone sat in the waiting room, each person lost in thought.

Patience was never one of Chayse's strong points, and he was pacing back and forth. "Will you please sit down before you wear a hole in the carpet?" Colar growled.

Dandre' threw his head back while laughing. "Why, little brother? Does it makes you nervous?"

"No, it makes me sick."

"I am sorry," Chayse said, coming to sit beside his brothers. "It's just that this baby is taking its time getting here."

Before Dandre' could respond, Christopher came out with a big smile on his face, announcing to everyone that he had a daughter. "Congratulations, son," Melody's father said as he gave Christopher a big hug.

Dr Ryan slapped him on the back. "Congrats, son."

"How is Melody?" Marconnets asked.

"She is fine," Chris replied.

"This baby is early!"

"Yes, we did not expect her for another two weeks."

Colar grinned. "I am ready to be an uncle," he said, winking at the others.

"What makes you so sure?" quipped his mother, Drusilla.

"Because I am the most charming of your sons, and my niece is going to take one look at me and fall hopelessly in love with me."

"Gosh, Colar. Your ego is astounding," Dandre' said.

"I am going to spoil her rotten!" He grinned while rocking on his heels.

"Have you decided on a name yet?" Governor Spencer asked.

"Yes. It's Rachel, after her grandmother."

"Oh, how sweet!" Andy said. "I know your grandmother will be thrilled to know that her first granddaughter is named after her."

Dandre' walked over to Andy and pulled her into his arms. "I can't wait to give you a baby. I have been dreaming about it ever since I first laid eyes on you."

Chuckling, Andy wrapped her arms around his neck and whispered, "Is that the reason why you never use any protection?"

"No. I wanted to go skin to skin with you," he said in a husky voice. "And besides, I wanted you to feel my release shot into your womb."

Before she could respond, Chayse said, "Hey, you two, knock it off!"

Dandre' said, "You are jealous," as he gently released Andy with a grin. He walked over to Christopher and hugged him.

"Congratulation," Andy said. "Are you happy?"

"Oh yes," Chris replied. "I am truly a blessed man. I have a gorgeous wife who just gave birth to the most beautiful baby girl, and I have a family that loves me. I have a lot to be thankful for."

Dandre' looked forward to when he would be alone again with Andy. As he watched her talk to his brother, he fantasised about all the naughty things he would do to her.

Colar was standing with his back towards the family. His hand was buried in his pocket as he stared out the window, deep in thought. More than once today, he found himself thinking of Paige and wondering what she was doing. Somehow he found his thoughts would stray towards her at the most unexpected times. He kept thinking about their night together and how amazing she was, even as a virgin.

Colar realised he wanted more of what they had shared that night. His body ached for Paige. Here he was with his family, celebrating a joyous occasion, and he was left with this desperate feeling—not just for any woman, but one in particular. After turning from the window and feeling a little disgusted, he walked towards the others, desperate to shake his melancholy feelings. "This calls for some champagne," he said.

"Yes," Chayse said, "but we are still at the hospital, and there is none available here."

"I think we should meet at Colar's later, to celebrate," Christopher said.

"Hey, where did you go?" Chayse asked Colar as they sat at the bar.

"Sorry. My mind drifted off," Colar told his brother.

"Yeah, I remember those days. I bet your mind is filled with a certain red-haired beauty," Christopher said with a grin.

"No, of course not. I was thinking about this business trip," Colar lied smoothly.

"When are you leaving?"

"Tomorrow. I won't be back for at least two weeks."

"But you will be back for Dandre's wedding," Chayse said.

"Of course I will be back in time for the wedding."

Christopher grinned and said, "He wouldn't miss the opportunity to walk with Paige."

Hissing his teeth, Colar said, "Whatever, man."

Maybe we could catch up with you. Anjou, the girls, and I are going shopping for the wedding while you are there."

"That would be great," Christopher said. "I wish Melody could go, but maybe after the wedding, I can take her to France."

"Seriously, Chris? You are disgustingly pleasant. What happened to the die-hard womaniser and workaholic?" Chayse asked.

"Melody happened. I did not know I could be so happy. If I am away from her for a night, I feel so empty," Chris said.

Colar gut-clenched at those words. *This is scary,* he thought. *What's happening to me?* He wasn't his brothers, and he would not allow himself to think about it. "I feel like an intruder when I am around you and Dandre' now," he said, feeling sorry for himself. He loved the women who were in his brothers' lives, but all this love was making him sick. It was if they were sharing some great secrets that he and Chayse couldn't possibly understand. "Whatever. You guys can come and throw your happiness in my face."

Chayse burst out laughing at the woebegone expression on his brother's face. "Stop whining," he jeered. "You could have the same thing with Paige. Take my advice and let down your defences. Maybe you could experience what Chris and Dandre' have."

"No, thank you. I will pass on that."

"That's what I said too. Let's see how long you last," Christopher said with a knowing look.

Christopher, Dandre', and Chayse took off. Colar tried to put Paige out of his mind while he tried focusing on his trip. He really did enjoy Spain; it was a beautiful place, and the dealers he was meeting with produced top-of-the-line vintage. The biggest expansion he was embarking on would consume him wholeheartedly, which would be a good thing.

Hissing his teeth in frustration, Colar slammed the pen down on his desk with far more force than was necessary. He had been in Spain for more than a week. Sitting behind his desk and reviewing documents was not enough to quell his bad mood. He couldn't believe he was still unable to get Paige out of his mind. Her scent caused his nostrils to flare and his groin to throb. *What the hell is wrong with me?* he wondered. Maybe he needed to get laid. But the thought of being with another woman did not appeal to him.

Several times he reached for the phone to call her, but each time he stopped. What excuse would he use? He was going home. He couldn't take being apart from her any longer. He still reassured himself that he simply needed to get her out of his system.

Andy and the girls had showed up, except for Paige. When he had asked about her, Andy told him she had some deadline to meet. Although he did not believe the excuse, he did not say anything. To his way of thinking, Paige was avoiding him. But who could blame her? He had taken off a few days to tour the city with them, but his smile had been fake, and his joy had been subdued. He continued to rationalise his frustration, and when he could not concentrate on the document he was reading, he decided to call it a day.

He was ready to head home. He'd find Paige and persuade her to go out with him. He couldn't get her off his mind, so the next best thing was to go home and see where things were going to lead. He had a real problem, though, because he did not do forever.

Andy stretched as the sunlight filtered through the window, waking her up. She had bought her condo two years after joining her family business. When she had first laid eyes on it, she knew this was the place for her, and she had fallen in love instantly. To her, it had been a safe haven from the craziness of corporate Jamaica, but now she was ready to move on with her life and embark on a new adventure with Dandre'. This place had been a dream. She lay there, enjoying the softness of her bed. She couldn't believe she had found love. After her horrific break-up with Adam, she had sworn that she would never let another man in her heart. Somehow, Dandre' had broken through her defences and captured her heart. In retrospect, she realised she had loved Adam with a young girl's love, which had grown from childhood friendship. But her love for Dandre' was from a woman who had finally stepped into her own and was no longer afraid to be vulnerable with another human being.

Humming softly, Andy jumped from her bed, quickly showered, got dressed, and headed for her car. Today, she and her sisters were going hiking. The morning started beautifully. There was a light breeze blowing over the island, and from time to time, there could be an unexpected downpour, which enabled the vegetation around Negril to stay lush and green, even in the middle of summer.

When Andy arrived at the designated spot she had agreed to meet her sisters, she parked her car and entered the building. "Good morning, all," she said.

"Morning, sis," they chorused. "Ready to go?"

"Yep."

As the girls exited the building, laughing and talking, they did not see the handsome stranger headed towards them. Marconnets turned around and collided with the man's solid chest, which sent her sprawling on her behind.

"Are you all right?" The deep baritone of his voice penetrated her fog-filled mind. Time stood still as she found herself gazing into eyes the colour of warm cherry. The stranger bent over her, extending his large hand. "Here." He pulled her to feet.

"Yes, I am fine," she snapped, more out of embarrassment.

"Excuse me?" the man said. "You are very rude. Next time, you should look where you are going!" With that, he strutted away.

Marconnets stared at his retreating backside.

"Are you OK?" Andy and Marche asked.

"Yes, I am fine," she said as she bent to retrieve her bag from the floor.

"If you are sure. Come on. Let's go," Marche said.

The girls headed up the trail. Marconnets could not help but wonder who the stranger was.

For more than two hours, the sisters continued their hiking trail. Finally panting, Marche said, "I am tired. Can we stop for a short rest?"

"Our destination is just ahead of us," Andy said. "We are less than five minutes away."

"OK, no problem. I think I can make it," Marche said with a smile.

"I know you can, sissy," Marconnets said.

After lunch, the girls wandered around the hiking ground, visiting different novelty shops and buying souvenirs, before heading back down the trail. "Are you feeling wedding jitters yet?" Melody asked Andy.

"A little." Andy glanced at her sister-in-law as she gently rocked her niece. "Is that normal?"

"Hell, yes," Melody replied. "When I was getting married to your future brother-in-law, I was a nut basket." She smiled. "I remember ruining my make-up because I was crying so hard. Finally, Daddy came in and sat, holding my hand and giving me reassurances that everything was going to be fine. You would never guess that a grown woman would be holding on to her father's hand as if it were a lifeline."

"Why were you crying?" Andy asked.

"I was scared that I was not good enough for Christopher."

"Wow," Andy said. "Who would have thought that? You always look so self-confident and in control. Girl, you had nothing to worry about. You had him eating out of the palm of your delicate hands." They laughed.

Melody said, "I wasn't so sure at the time. I wanted everything to be perfect. As you can see, he is quiet a catch."

"Yes he is—and so are you. He is blessed to be married to you."

"Thank you," Melody said as she leaned over to hug Andy.

"Women," Christopher said, sighing to himself. "They are so emotional." He silently walked away from the door before either woman realised he was eavesdropping on their conversation. He grinned from ear to as he walked into the den where his brothers were sitting.

"Why the big smile?" Chayse asked.

Sticking his chest out, Chris said, "My wife thinks I'm quite the catch."

"Really?" Colar chimed. "And I'm the one with the ego?"

"I did not make that up," Christopher chirruped. "I heard her telling Andy."

Dandre' high-fived Christopher as they exchanged a knowing glance.

Hissing his teeth, Colar said, "Let's watch the football game." He took a swallow of his beer.

"So who do you think is going to win the game?" Tyler asked. "Brazil or Argentina?"

"I would say Brazil," Chayse replied.

"Although both teams are good, I agree with Chayse," Colar replied.

Pretty soon the men were lost in the game, yelling and

screaming as they cheered for their respective teams. When Brazil scored yet another goal, Christopher swore at the TV screen as if the goalkeeper could hear him. At halftime, he was ready to climb up the wall. Dandre' grinned like the cat that swallowed the canary, enjoying his brother's misery. There was nothing like a good game to get Chris riled up.

At halftime, Andy walked in with a tray of refreshments, placing the tray on a side table. Dandre' reached out and snagged her around the waist, pulling her onto his lap. "Thank you, beautiful," he said as he nipped her earlobe.

"You are welcome," she breathed.

"Happy?" Dandre' asked.

"Very."

He bent and told her just what he intended to do when he got back to his house. Andy blushed.

Melody gave her a knowing look. Are you OK, Andy?"

Andy smiled as she glanced at everyone in the room. "Yes. I couldn't be better."

Andy lay snuggled in Dandre's arms. After he'd made love to her three times, she had drifted off to sleep. He had been watching her since. She was a silent sleeper; the gentle rise and fall of her chest was the only indication that she was breathing. He gently wrapped a handful of her hair around his hand as he inhaled. He liked the smell of her hair; it had a citrusy smell. But when it came to Anjou, what was there not to like about her? He could feel his manhood stir as intense desire for her roused within him.

Dandre' gently eased out of bed so as not to wake her. He glanced over his shoulder as he left the room. He knew if he stayed, he would make love to her again, and she needed her rest.

When Andy woke up in the morning, she was violently ill. *A sure sign that I ate something last night that did not agree with me,* Andy thought as she showered and dresses.

Dandre' was already up, and she went into the kitchen. She grimaced when she caught the smell of steamed Callaloo and codfish. Mrs Reid looked at her with concern. "Are you all right, my dear?" she enquired.

"Just a little queasy," she explained. "Something I ate, I imagine."

"If you say so," the housekeeper said, grinning at her.

It was several minutes before the import of her teasing comment registered to Andy's consciousness. When it did, a bright flush stained her cheeks. She sat down on a nearby chair. Andy's legs were shaking not from fear but excitement. *Dear God, I had not thought of that! What if I'm pregnant?* They'd had unprotected sex numerous of times, but she'd never gotten pregnant. With just three weeks before their wedding, she hoped that it was not so. It was not that she didn't want to be pregnant. She was worried her dress might not fit. She knew Dandre' would be elated, but for now, she would keep her suspicions to herself until she could confirm it.

Dandre' walked in a few minutes later, and Mrs Ettie served breakfast. Andy was relieved when she was given only two slices of toast. Dandre' raised his eyebrows. "I am not hungry," Andy said, avoiding his eyes. She was grateful when Mrs Ettie kept quiet, merely exchanging a thoughtful glance with her over Dandre's head.

Later, when Dandre' left for the office, Andy thanked the housekeeper for not saying anything. "I want it to be a surprise when I tell him on our honeymoon," Andy explained.

CHAPTER 12

Dandre' stood at the front of the church. As he watched, Andy was escorted down the aisle by her father. He thought the same thing now as he had the night he'd first seen her at the Sunset Negril: Anjou was the most beautiful and enchanting creature that he had ever laid eyes on.

He was so lost in his own thoughts as he watched her approach that he was not aware a tear slipped down his cheeks until Christopher, his best man, whispered, "Are you all right?"

"Yes, I am fine," he replied. "Why do you ask?"

"It's just that you are crying," Christopher said, grinning.

Dandre' replied, "These are tears of happiness, bro. I am one of the luckiest men alive."

"That you are." The two brothers exchanged knowing glances before turning their attention back to Andy.

"By the power vested in me, I now pronounce you husband and wife," the minister said. "Mr Neilson, you may now kiss your bride."

"With pleasure," Dandre' said as he pulled Andy into his arms, devouring her mouth with an intensity that he felt all the way to his toes. Forgetting where he was, Dandre' feasted on Andy's lips like there was no tomorrow. He did not hear the minister clear his throat.

Tyler tap him on his shoulder and whispered, "Damn, Dandre', you are still in the church." Dandre' chuckled, took one last lick at her mouth, and stepped back.

Cheers went up as the minister said, "Ladies and gentleman, it is with great pleasure that I present to you Mr and Mrs Dandre' Roland Neilson."

Andy, Dandre', and their wedding party had taken a multitude of pictures in the beautiful ballroom of the Royal Crown Hotel, which she had designed. Not only was their home finished, but also the restaurant, hotel, and resort. Andy smiled at the thought that theirs would be the first of many wedding receptions to take place here. They danced to "It Seems Like Forever I Have Waited for You".

"You look lovely, my bride," Dandre' purred in her hair as they swayed to the music.

"And you, my prince, are extremely breathtaking," she said, resting her cheeks against his chest. She could feel the strong beat of his heart. He was dressed in an Ecru suit with a peach bowtie and cummerbund. She was wearing an exquisite, sleeveless, elaborately beaded, form-fitting wedding gown that featured an illusion neckline and low sheer back with beautiful embroidery. The back was finished with a Simi-chapel trail. The dress was the same colour as Dandre's suit. On her feet, she wore glass slippers.

They danced for what seem like an eternity before Dandre' felt a light tap on his back. "I think it's my turn to dance with my new daughter-in-law," Dr Neilson said, grinning.

"Sure, Dad," Dandre' said as her relinquished his hold on Anjou. After that, everything got amazingly boisterous and wild. Jamaicans liked to party and celebrate joyous occasions. Andy danced with Dandre's, brothers, cousins, and uncles who were present. The sound of the music was sensual, exotic, and lively.

Later, Andy felt like she was in a dream as she changed out of her dress. She said as much to her sisters. Gail said, "We are so happy for you, Andy. May you always reflect the glow and happiness that is emanating from you tonight."

"Thank you," she said, hugging her friend. "I am delighted that you are here to share this special occasion with me."

Dandre' lifted his wife of five hours and carried her over the threshold of their honeymoon suite. Using his feet, he pushed the door close as he placed her on her feet. Andy turned around and realised the lighting was extremely low. There were scented candles burning everywhere. She looked down at the floor and saw rose petals everywhere. On a low table beside the huge four-poster bed was an ice bucket with a bottle of champagne. The surface of the bed was also covered with the petals of the exotic tropical flower known as Duranta Repens.

Andy gasped as she saw the scene before her. Desire danced across her skin as she stared into the golden depths of her husband's eyes. Dandre' began to undress her slowly. Words were unnecessary because they had created a language of their own with their eyes and touch. Dandre' nuzzled her neck as he rained butterfly kisses on the parts of her body he exposed. He purred against her delicate skin, and his lips latched onto her throat, drawing lovingly on her. He unzipped her dress, sliding it from her shoulders. The garment pooled around her ankle like a soft cloud. He carried her to the bed and he gently laid on it. He took a step back, his gaze never leaving her as he began to undress.

Andy watched in fascination as he stripped for her. Standing before her was a magnificent male in all his glory. Andy thought for the millionth time that his form was perfect, and he was truly beautiful. She held out her hand, and he took it. "Make love to me, Dandre'. Take me to the stars," she whispered.

Dandre' bent over her and captured her lips in a searing kiss. "You are in my blood, mon cheri," he breathed as his tongue danced with hers. Her eyes closed as a heady sensation began to wash over her. He worked his way down to her breasts and captured one jutting peak in his hot mouth. He licked and sucked to his heart's content. A small sound issued from her lips, and her skin tingle everywhere he caressed.

"Dandre' …" she breathed. She placed her arms on his upper chest, feeling the satiny texture of his warm skin.

Leaning back on his heel, Dandre' reached for the bottle of exotic oil. He poured some in his large hands and blew on it to warm it before massaging the oil into her skin with long, even strokes. Everywhere his hands caressed, her body rose to meet his touch. Soon her body was glistening in the candlelight. He reached over to a small jar of honey. "Close your eyes, sweetheart," he purred.

Andy closed her eyes, as he requested. Dandre' dipped his index finger in the honey and gently outlined her lips. "Mmm," she muttered. He lathered every inch of her body. He leaned over her, his long hair brushing against her breasts in a feather-light caress. Then with long, slow, sensuous licks, he used his tongue to remove the honey from her body, all the way to the soles of her feet. Andy began to writhe beneath him as liquid fire danced in her veins. She moaned and begged him for more.

He used the tip of his tongue to tease the seam of her womanhood. After raising her leg, he licked and gently nipped her inner thigh before moving to the junction of her legs. Dandre' used his mouth to caress her feminine core. Andy spread her legs to give him greater access. Using his tongue, he stroked her inside. Andy reared up off the bed as the first wave of ecstasy hit her. "Oh," she moaned.

Dandre' used his muscular legs to spread her, and he penetrated her deeply in one swift thrust. The sensation was so acute that it triggered another orgasm. Andy wrapped her legs around his waist as he went deeper. She moved to the rhythm that he established. He was a dominant yet tender and passionate masterful. He varied the depths of his thrust as he moved within her body. His movement and thrust had a spellbinding effect on her. Andy was stunned by the intensity of his skill as a lover.

Dandre' withdrew and turned her on her side before swiftly entering her again. His passion was a raging storm. She looked in his passionate, glazed eyes as he bit her shoulder. Andy pulled him to her and held him. She loved him holding nothing back, and she gave it all to him as she responded to his untamed thrusts and passion-filled cries, which triggered yet another orgasm.

Andy purred deep in her throat as Dandre' hit her G spot, throwing his head back. Andy's inner muscles began to milk him for an orgasm of gigantic proportions. He cried, "Anjou, my Anjou, your love is sweeter than honey and more intoxicating than wine." In that moment, Dandre', the master of seduction, knew that he was truly captured by this raven-haired beauty whose name meant wine.

They made love practically the whole night. Dandre' was such a passionate and considerate lover that he gave more than he could ever receive.

When she woke up in the morning, the sun was shining through the window, and its rays danced across her face. Andy remembered the scandalous things her husband had done to her throughout the night with his hands, lips, tongue, and teeth. He had licked her from head to toe. She blushed as she also remembered the way she had responded wantonly to him. Towards the break of dawn, she'd taken him by surprise, turning the tables. She could still see the look in his eyes as she straddled him and gave him the ride of his life—something she had enjoyed immensely She moaned aloud as she recalled him sprawled on his back under her. The look of raw desire had radiated from him as he'd encouraged her, whispering naughty things to her in French.

Dandre' was sitting at the foot of the bed, gazing at her as he watched the play of emotions across her face. "Good morning," she said shyly.

"Good morning, my blushing bride," he drawled lazily. "How are you feeling?"

"I am …" Before she could finish her sentence, a wave of nausea hit her. She leapt from the bed and made a dash for the bathroom.

Dandre' rushed in behind his wife. "Oh my God. Anjou, are you OK?"

It was some time before she lifted her head from the toilet. "Yes, I am fine. It seems like Junior is rather impatient and wants to make his presence known to you."

"Is this what I think it is?" Dandre' said, smiling. "Am I going to be a father? Why didn't you tell me?"

"I was going to tell you," she said, smiling weakly. "I wasn't sure. It was only confirmed a few days ago, so I decided to tell you on our honeymoon."

Dandre' lifted her to her feet and wrapped her in his warm embrace. "Oh, darling. This is some of the best news I have heard! I have been praying that you would be pregnant. I know we have never really discussed children, but you do want to have them, right?"

"Them?" Andy said. "How much is them?"

"Six or seven."

"Are you kidding me?" she said in mock indignation.

Dandre' picked her up in his arms and began twirling her around.

"What are you doing?" she said, laughing.

"I am doing my happy dance!"

"Put me down. You are going to make me dizzy!"

Dandre' walked over to the bed and gently laid her down. He picked up her left hand and placed a warm, tender kiss on her palm as he gazed into her lovely hazel eyes. "From the moment I met you, I knew we were destined to be together. I knew I would father your children. The problem was I couldn't tell you. You were running so fast that I had to devise a plan. That's when I approached you to design the plan for the house, spa, restaurants, and resort. I was desperate, so I was willing to do everything and anything to get your attention. I knew once that was done, I hoped to get you to fall in love with me."

"You were mighty sure of yourself," she said, poking him gently in the chest.

Dandre' chuckled. "Believe me—it was not an easy feat to accomplish, mon cheri. You were most difficult to persuade." He laid his hand on her stomach. "Do you think it's a girl?"

"No, I think it's a boy," she said. "Either way, it does not matter. Whether boy or girl, we are going to create some beautiful babies."

"So does that mean you are going to give me at soccer team?" he teased.

"I will give you as many babies as you want, my prince. Your wish is my command."

He kissed her and then lapped languorously, feeling the uneven beat of her heart. He groaned her name and buried his face in her hair. His arms went around her, imprisoning her against his aroused body. His mouth found her throat and explored the soft, satin skin. The rough passion brought a hectic and feverish throb to his pulse. He raised his head reluctantly, his lambent eyes glittering fiercely. "I want you, Anju," he told her. "If you don't stop me now, there is no way I will be able to stop myself."

"Who says I want you to stop?" she purred seductively, capturing his mouth in a hot kiss.

He pulled back. "But what about breakfast? Surely you must be hungry."

Andy laughed. "It can wait. Yes, I am hungry—but not for food … My appetite calls for a certain golden-eyed rogue named Dandre'." She eased the silk robe from his broad shoulders as she explored his massive chest, raining butterfly kisses on him before capturing a hard nipple between her teeth. She gently bit him with just enough pressure to create a sting before licking it with her tongue to give a pleasurable sensation. Dandre' growled deep in his throat.

Andy worked her way down to his navel, using her hand to caress his inner thighs. She flipped him on his back—a move that caught him by surprise. While kneeling between his legs, Andy took his big shaft in her mouth as she licked and sucked to her heart's content.

Finally Dandre' could stand no more. In a quick manoeuvre, he had her on her back, penetrating her swiftly and deeply. Andy cried out at the exquisite sensation. "Say you like it," Dandre' purred in her ear as he began to move within her. Andy rode the waves of passion with her husband, dancing to a music that they had created. When their release came simultaneously, they both plunged into the abyss of total satisfaction.

It was late afternoon when she woke. After looking around, she realised she was alone. She lay there for a few minutes before finally heading to the bathroom. Andy took a leisurely bath, dressed, and went in search of her husband.

Dandre' was sitting in the living room of their suite, watching a game. "Hi, you are awake. Are you hungry?" he asked.

"I am starving," she replied.

"Would you like to go out to eat, or do you prefer room service?"

"I think I will stay in. Besides, we've already missed most of the activities," she said, yawning.

"Come sit beside me," he said. Andy did as he requested, and Dandre' lifted her feet, placed them in his lap, and gently massaged them.

After they ate, Dandre' suggested they go for a walk. He held her hand as they leisurely strolled through the grounds of the resort where they were staying.

"Hawaii is such a beautiful place," Andy mused as she admired their surroundings.

"Yes, it is," Dandre' replied. "But not as beautiful as you, mon cheri."

Her chin rested in his hand as he kissed her forehead. Andy shivered as his lips touched hers. She wondered whether he would affect her like this for the rest of their lives. It never ceased to amaze her that with just one look, those eyes of his could get her hot and bothered.

Dandre' picked up on her thoughts and said, "You do have the same effect on me, my love. No other woman has ever affected me the way you do. You make me weak at the knees. My sweet Anjou, if I am away from you for more than a few minutes, I can't stop thinking about you. I carry you in my spirit. When you smile, my world is complete. Andy, you are my world. I can't live without you. For the rest of my life, I will show you just how much you mean to me."

Tears of joy welled up in her eyes as she took his beautiful face between her hands. "Oh, Dandre'. You are my life. I never thought I would find love after what I went through with Adam, and I was scared to let another man in because I believed all of them were the same. But then you came along, and you broke through the barriers and demolished all my defences. You taught me to believe in love again. When I was a little girl, I used to believe in fairy tales, and I dreamed about being a princess. My knight in shining armour would ride on a beautiful white stallion. Those dreams were dashed to pieces when my ex-fiancé's family rejected me because of the colour of my skin. Today, I am grateful that I did not married Adam because if I had, I would not have met the most amazing man who ever graced the planet." Andy chuckled. "Besides, who wants to be a part of a family that is so vain and superficial?"

Dandre' hugged her. "He was a fool to let you go. One

man's foolishness is another man's gain. I am truly sorry that you had to encounter such ignorance and stupidity. If he did not play the fool, I would not be here with you." He released her. "Come on. Let's finish our walk. Tonight, there is a luau on the beach. Would you like to go?"

"Most definitely," she said, grinning back at him.

Seven Months Later

Anjou laughed with Dandre' as she surveyed the large crowd of people. The recently completed Royal Crown Hotel, owned by her husband—this was quite a christening indeed. "Are you sure Acquel will be safe with your father?" she asked anxiously.

"Of course," Dandre' said, laughing. "He raised four boys, remember?"

She focused with motherly concern on the other side of the room. Dr Juan Neilson was proudly showing off his three-month-old grandson to his friends.

"As your mother reminded us, they have held far more babies than we have," Dandre' said, laughing.

"Maybe, but none of them have been our baby," she said. "I think I'd better go get him. He is beginning to look fretful, and he never finished his last bottle …"

"Talk about doting fathers. Look at you!" Marconnets teased as they watched Andy hurrying away towards her son.

"I always knew Anjou would be a very good mother," Marche said.

Dandre' smiled as he watched his wife expertly hold their son, who'd been born seven months after their marriage. Dandre' was the most wonderful father and husband, and he was a considerate lover.

Andy gave a small sigh as she handed her son to Mama Nadia. A look darkened her eyes, which he recognised immediately. If his grandmother was surprised that she was suddenly handed her grandson while Andy insisted that there was something she needed to discuss with her husband in private, she gave no sign of it. Instead, Nadia joined Andy's mother, with whom she shared a very close bond.

"Anjou, are you sure about this?" Dandre' asked as she led him to one of the most luxurious bedrooms and locked the door.

"Why not?" she teased him. "We own the hotel, and we are married. Right now, I want you so much."

Dandre' sighed as his lips found the exquisitely tender cord in her throat that always responded to his lips.

"Oh, Dandre'," she breathed. "Make love to me now."

He moved his head down towards her mouth, which opened sweetly for him. "With pleasure, my darling." He allowed himself to be carried away on the tidal waves of unbridled passion.